"Oh, Tony, let's not argue."

Lizzie walked towards him, speaking softly and searching his face. "You've changed a little. I..."

Sir Antony felt a constriction in his throat. She was so close, so beautiful. "You haven't."

"We've...I've missed you."

"I've missed you, too."

Another step closer and she could feel herself against him. The reaction was instantaneous. Her breathing quickened sharply. She lifted her tingling fingertips to stroke his cravat. Turning her face up to his, she closed her eyes and waited.

Slowly and gently, he pushed her away.

Suprise was quickly followed by anger. Lizzie's back straightened; her voice grew ice cold. "I don't believe we have anything further to discuss. I'm sure you know the way out."

He had no choice, but as he left Tony cursed his wretched pride. He did not see the tears that glistened in Lizzie's eyes.

LADY
ELIZABETH

LINELL ANSTON

TORONTO • NEW YORK • LONDON
AMSTERDAM • PARIS • SYDNEY • HAMBURG
STOCKHOLM • ATHENS • TOKYO • MILAN

Published May 1990

ISBN 0-373-31126-5

Printed in U.S.A.

CHAPTER ONE

"REGGIE! Have you been staring out that window since I left?"

"Umph?" Reginald Croyton turned a vacant gaze upon his sister.

Standing in the library doorway, she was dressed stunningly in a light brown walking gown. The full skirts fell almost to the floor and barely covered the yellow satin slipper tapping impatiently upon the carpet. Just returned from outdoors, she still wore a loose-fitting pelisse about her shoulders, and she pushed this away from her hips in irritation. The dress beneath was a high-waisted muslin tunic above a pale yellow silk chemise. A large leghorn hat, plumed with ostrich feathers, sat at a rakish tilt upon her head but did not entirely conceal her golden curls.

For two years, as the celebrated Toast of the ton, she had captivated hearts of both young and old; yet the beauty of her face was presently marred by the stern expression she bestowed upon her brother.

Unperturbed by her censure, Lord Croyton gazed nonchalantly at his younger sister.

"Had you gone somewhere?" he asked.

"You know very well I've been to the milliner's," she replied as her toe increased its restless dance upon the rug.

His lordship's omnipresent quizzing glass shot up, and she now found herself the subject of close scrutiny.

"And what a charming hat you've chosen, Lizzie," came the final verdict. "It quite becomes you."

Lizzie swallowed the retort which rose instantly to her lips. The hat he found so charming upon her was the one he himself had bought her less than a month ago.

Lord Croyton, having given what he felt to be the appropriate response, had already returned to the window.

Lizzie sighed, for she knew her brother all too well and recognized his mood instantly; his mind was elsewhere. There would be no talking sense to him until he wished it.

The sixth Earl of Drenview was, at the young age of twenty-five, the most eligible catch of the British peerage. The five years separating brother and sister did nothing to diminish the twinlike quality of the pair for, like herself, Lord Croyton was tall, slender and fairhaired with the finest of features.

Closer inspection would show the resemblance faltered. There was rarely doubt or indecision in the sharp, clear blue eyes of Lady Elizabeth. They sparkled with laughter and flashed her displeasure; her face revealed each passing emotion. The earl was not so volatile. His closest friends were often heard to remark that his face was devoid of all expression, except perhaps boredom. Lazy eyelids hung above pale blue, perpetually glassy eyes.

The difference was further accentuated when they spoke. The precise, clipped tones of Lady Elizabeth were the antithesis of the languid drawl her brother affected. Lizzie loved to laugh, which she did freely without the simpering and posturing so fashionable among the well-behaved young ladies of Quality.

Lizzie was always on the move. Unbounding energy sent her flying from Assembly to rout to garden party without a break in momentum. Older matrons were known to remark, albeit in hushed tones, that Lady Elizabeth was "rather wild." They could wish she were more like the earl, but they agreed that it was to be expected since she was young, rich and beautiful—a dreadful combination, especially in a girl without proper chaperonage.

This was no reflection upon Lord Croyton, it was understood by all, as someone of his lordship's demeanour could not possibly be expected to exert any authority over a strong-willed, wayward sister. He was far too indulgent of the girl's whims. Otherwise, however could he have permitted her to race her gig against Lord Bettlely's? Not unusual behaviour for the high-spirited of the time, assuredly—but through Hyde Park at the height of the afternoon? It was even hinted, by those who claimed to know, that his lordship had placed a sizeable wager upon his sister's successful conclusion of the race, and that she won did nothing to quell such absurd gossip.

Rumours aside, the consensus was that Lord Croyton was simply too sedate and well-mannered and, put bluntly, not sufficiently "all there" to keep adequate rein upon a young girl of such youthful exuberance. A heartfelt sigh of relief would be heaved by all of London society the moment Lady Elizabeth Croyton chose a husband.

Until then, such chaos in the order of things could be overlooked with indulgent condescension. For when she was on her best behaviour, Lady Elizabeth was witty, charming and an asset at any dull affair. The hostesses of London could be guaranteed success if she deigned to appear, and no Assembly could be denied complete success if brother and sister arrived together.

When the mood possessed him, Lord Croyton loved to talk, and it was never what he said that amused and delighted, but how he said it.

He was not in the mood at present.

Lizzie removed her pelisse and tossed it and her hat onto the nearest chair. Her gaze fell upon the pile of mail sitting neglected on the desk.

"Why, you haven't even gone through the morning mail. Honestly, Reggie! I do think you could try to be more responsible. Must I do everything about this place? I don't object ordinarily, but only this morning Childers came to me and . . ."

She raised her eyes from the mail in her hand to study her errant brother. He was gazing out the window, tapping his lower lip with his glass and not paying the slightest attention to her.

"What can be of such interest out there?" she asked, and strode forward purposefully to peer through the window.

The Croyton town residence was situated in that prestigious corner of London known as Hanover Square. Not only was it so conveniently located to the hub of fashionable society, but it commanded a remarkable view upon this quarter of the world from the very library window at which Lizzie stood. If there had been any activity upon the street, it would not have gone unnoticed by the vigilant pair.

"There's not a soul on the street." She returned to the mail in disgust, and her expression immediately changed to one of joy. "Look! Another letter from Tony!" She dropped to the window seat and waved the letter at her brother. "Open it! It's addressed to you."

Lord Croyton absently took the proffered envelope, glanced at the address and returned it. "Tony addresses the envelopes to me," he replied plaintively, "but he writes to you. The pleasure is all yours."

Lizzie needed no further encouragement and tore open the seal breathlessly. "I wonder why he's writing again so soon. You don't suppose anything can have happened? Oh, I can just feel it must be something dreadful for him to write twice in one month. And to think I haven't even finished my letter to him. I was waiting to tell him about Aunt Martie's soirée tonight, but now..."

The recital stopped as she quickly scanned the first few lines of the precious missive and the furrow of concentration on her brow was quickly eclipsed by a smile of delight.

"Oh, Reggie! This is marvellous! He's coming home!"

The news drew an unexpected response from Lord Croyton. "I knew it!" he cried triumphantly.

Wonder and disappointment mingled in the girl's voice. "Why, Reggie, how could you know it?"

"Why, m'dear Lizzie, by the cut of his coat," his lordship replied succinctly.

His sister's confused expression demanded further elaboration, and he stretched his tall frame to its full height to add emphasis to his words.

"You have thought me idle," he protested, "but, in fact, I have been testin' my ability to recognize members of our privileged class simply by the style of their wardrobe. I pride myself—" which was obvious from his tone "—that in this case, although I only caught a glimpse, and from the back, mind you, I knew it was he." He paused for thought and added, "I never shall understand how he can abide those tight waistcoats."

Familiar with the vagaries of her beloved sibling, Lizzie resigned herself to the inevitable. "What are you going on so about?" She asked.

"Harvey Forbisher" was the placid response.

A vision of this middle-aged gentleman appeared before her. "What does Harvey Forbisher have to do with anything?"

"Actually—" her brother considered the question in all earnestness "—I don't suppose he has much to do with anythin'—that is if he can manage it—except, it would appear, the good countess." He waved his glass toward the window.

It was indeed Harvey Forbisher scurrying away from the door of the next town house. Mr. Forbisher was a respectable, and therefore, in Lizzie's opinion, a dull individual. Added to that, he was an obnoxious gossip and possessed the worst possible taste in clothes. At present a garishly striped green-and-maroon waistcoat barely covered his over-large stomach. His stocking net breeches were a shade of lime green which Lizzie had never before seen and which she fervently hoped never to see again. They were fastened over his stockings with the largest knee buckles imaginable. To top off this spectacle, the coat he wore was almost the same colour as his breeches, with buttons that matched the knee buckles in sheer size and opulence.

Lizzie stole a sly glance at her brother's own impeccable figure. In comparison, the earl was dressed quite simply. He wore no coat and his waistcoat was of the smart Newmarket style, double-breasted and square cut. It was a rich Oriental silk brocade of gold and silver. Buckskin breeches beautifully offset the gold colour in the waistcoat and were close fitting to show off a well-proportioned leg. The ruffles at his wrist and collar were of the finest lace available and even the eyeglass he so carelessly dangled was the best quality and fashioned from the purest gold.

Lizzie returned to her contemplation of Mr. Forbisher. His presence would generate no comment ordinarily, except that Lord DeBoeulle, whose house Mr. Forbisher was leaving, was known to be in the North Country on business. Mr. Forbisher did seem, Lizzie reflected, to be in an amazing hurry for such a large man in such tight breeches. He glanced up and down the street furtively.

"I wonder what *pressin'* business they could have had to discuss," Lord Croyton murmured suggestively.

"Oh, you do have an imagination," she replied, giggling at the insinuation. "You're not suggesting..."

His lordship leaned down to his sister's ear. "Witness the pitiful state of his cravat."

"Oh!"

Belatedly remembering that her conduct was not befitting a young lady of Quality, Lizzie spun from the window conscience-stricken.

"How simply odious!" she scolded. "Spying on your neighbors so! You ought to be ashamed. And you've distracted me from my letter," she added, pouting prettily.

Lord Croyton made a graceful leg. "Forgive me. What does your beloved Tony have to say for himself?"

"Our beloved Tony is coming home!" She laughed brightly and scanned the letter while he ensconced himself in a nearby chair. "Listen to this! He writes...oh, where is it?...ah...here.

"I have decided that it cannot serve my purpose to remain in America. I have, therefore, made arrangements to sail on the first available ship home. I should not be surprised if I reach you before this letter, as I sail in two weeks. But I feel compelled to write; in fact, my conscience demands it.''

She faltered at these words and continued more slowly.

''Forgive me if I did not tell you sooner or if I have not been completely truthful to you about my situation. It is only that your own letters contained such gaiety and life that I could not bring myself to destroy the few bright moments they gave me in this miserable place.''

''I told you he writes to you,'' Lord Croyton reiterated.
''Sssh!

''I have not been successful. I have not accomplished what I expected. I have sold my father's holdings here and even so I must return to England with less than when I departed. I will understand your anger at my deception; indeed, I fully expect it. I have committed an unforgivable act by misleading you and I have further compounded the error by ever presenting myself as being suitable.''

Her voice decreased steadily in volume and now she fell silent, furiously reading ahead.

''Reggie! Do you hear this?'' she demanded loudly.

''Contrary to popular opinion, m'dear, I'm not deaf,'' he replied.

''I cannot believe this! He's crying off! I never thought he could be so... so despicable!''

"Sink me, have I missed something? Terribly short-sighted of me, but I don't recall your being engaged." Lord Croyton watched his sister rise in fury and pace the width of the room. "Perhaps I'm being old-fashioned, but shouldn't I remember giving my approval?" he asked. "Now that is something I feel certain I would remember."

"No, we're not engaged. But we have an understanding—and now this!" She tossed the offending letter aside and continued her trek across the floor. "He should know that I don't care that he has no money. I shall have money enough for both of us. And as far as people thinking him a fortune hunter—well, that is simply too ridiculous to countenance! I have certainly never cared about what other people might think!"

One glance at her set mouth and glittering eyes was enough to warn even the inexperienced that there was more forthcoming. Lord Croyton waited silently and was soon rewarded for his patience.

"To think he could write such!" exploded Lizzie. "He imagines my anger! He fully expects it! Pray tell, what else could he expect? I," she pronounced emphatically, "could expect such stupidity from you perhaps, but *Tony*?"

His lordship opened his mouth to respond to this obviously unjust criticism but thought better of it. He was, however, galvanized into speech by the next remark.

"Reggie, you must take action!" She came to an abrupt halt before his chair, hands firmly planted upon her hips.

Lord Croyton shuddered perceptibly. "And what type of action must I take?" he asked weakly, gazing up into his sister's fiery eyes.

"It's obvious. You must go to Bristol immediately. Explain to this...this idiot everything that I have said and make him come to his senses."

Pent-up breath escaped the earl's lungs. "Thank you, Lizzie," he murmured. "I thought for certain I should have to challenge the chap to a duel. Which I shouldn't wish to do—not that I wouldn't defend your honour, if I had to—it's just that—dash it, the fellow is my best friend. And since you're not officially engaged—I never gave my consent, that I remember, that is—I should have a devil of a time comin' up with a reason."

"Duel him?" She scoffed. "Of course I wouldn't want you to duel him. He's a far better shot than you will ever be and as for swords...well, Reggie, I have more faith in your luck than your ability."

"I am monstrous lucky, aren't I?" His lordship concurred happily.

Lizzie's mind moved to other matters. She crossed the room and rang the servants' bell determinedly. "You will leave for Bristol tonight," she declared.

Now her brother squirmed violently. "Tonight? Do you think it necessary? Tony does write that he is returning to London, doesn't he? Frankly, I cannot see the purpose to my travellin' halfway 'cross country on the off chance of meetin' someone who's comin' here."

"He said his ship was leaving two weeks from when he sent the letter, which means it should arrive within the next few days. You will be there with plenty of time to spare. Explain to Sir Antony Russelford how silly he is being and return here with him. Simple enough. I think even you could manage it."

Lord Croyton took no offense at his sister's blunt expression. "Your confidence in my ability overwhelms me, dear sister, but I am bewildered by your time schedule. Give me a moment to consider—I'm certain it's flawed.''

"Nonsense." Lizzie watched him sink into deep concentration and her eyes travelled to the letter lying rejected on the floor. "Oh, Tony, why must you be this way," she murmured. "Reggie, I could never explain my reasons but I do need your help desperately with this. Something needs to be done."

Any further contemplation was interrupted by the arrival of their butler.

"Childers," Lizzie began briskly, "his lordship will be leaving immediately for Bristol. See that his carriage is brought round and inform Roberts."

"Certainly, my lady."

If Childers felt any surprise at this uncharacteristic request, he gave no indication and ignored the seated figure, directing his question to Lady Elizabeth. "May I ask if his absence will be a prolonged one?"

"A week . . . two at the most."

He nodded stoically, noted the good lady's agitation and the earl's own preoccupation and left to carry out the orders in his customarily efficient manner.

The moment the butler departed, Lizzie turned once again to her brother and pleaded, "When you arrive in Bristol you must wait for his ship. Talk to him, Reggie. He'll listen to you."

Lord Croyton sighed but restated his feelings patiently. "I cannot think this trip necessary. Given enough time, the fellow will come to you."

"I will not have him thinking that this silliness of his means so much," she said emphatically. "If you absolutely refuse to go, I shall simply have to go myself."

"Oh, dear, I cannot think that would serve," Lord Croyton replied. "In fact, I am quite certain that such a plan would be most improper. I should have to go with you, in any case."

"Then you will go," Lizzie said with a smile.

"I fear I cannot think of a way out of it," admitted his lordship as he stood. "Yes, I shall go. But I'll wager 'twill be for naught."

"Oh, Reggie! I knew you would help!"

His sister's exuberance took the form of a most constricting hug and the earl stepped back quickly.

"Pray contain yourself, Lizzie!" he cried. "You've almost ruined my cravat."

"You will have to change it anyway," she declared, laughing at his fastidiousness. "Childers should have everything ready within the hour."

Lord Croyton's eyes widened in surprise. "An hour? Sink me, Lizzie, would you have me leave without supper?"

"You may eat along the way, if you must. It's important that you leave immediately. You wouldn't want to take the chance of missing him."

Giving this comment his full consideration, his lordship frowned. "No, I suppose not. But, damme, I still think there's something wrong with your logic. I cannot seem to put my finger on it, but no matter, it will come to me."

"There is nothing wrong with my logic." She edged him closer to the door and commanded, "Now, go and change."

Although Childers reserved to himself all theories regarding his master's unusual behaviour, it cannot be said the rest of the household followed his stoic example. News that Lord Croyton was leaving immediately for Bristol spread like wildfire. His lordship *never* did anything *immediately*. This was one of the earl's traits, in fact, which endeared him to his staff. He had been known in the past to take four weeks to plan and pack for a three-week holiday in the country. The unexpectedness of this new eccentricity sent the household into a frenzy of activity.

There was a consensus that something was decidedly amiss, but the nature of that something was a matter of much argument. After several heated discussions, it was grudgingly agreed that Cook was correct when she pronounced that his lordship had finally lost whatever sense the Good Lord had seen fit to give him.

The credit for rousing the bewildered servants went to Childers. That acerbic soul, with a lifetime's experience in the service of Quality and twenty years spent in this somnolent household, found nothing to disrupt his belief that there was no understanding the upper classes. They lived by different rules, if one could say they lived by any rules at all, which was doubtful. One accepted that fact and carried on. Childers was thankful in many ways for the undisturbed routine of life to which he had become accustomed. It was a privilege to serve in a household comprising two young persons and not have to deal with the inconveniences which such service usually entailed. If he must now pay for that privilege, they would not find him lacking.

With the firmness of an army officer, Childers coddled the staff through the first wave of shock and propelled them into action. He even managed to spur Cook to the preparation of a light supper for his lordship. Childers had his own opinion of the quality of food to be found upon the road: it was not fit to feed to pigs.

So it was that within the hour, Lord Croyton's carriage was brought around, beautifully equipped with a superb set of matched greys, and loaded in a trice with all the baggage containing everything his lordship would need—and certainly more than he would ever want—for his two weeks' absence. Lord Croyton was dressed, fed and put on his way to Bristol. If he felt like a boy being packed off to his first day of the school term, he didn't mention it. It is doubtful that he paid attention to the flurry of activity surrounding him. He certainly gave no indication, but this, in itself, was not unusual.

CHAPTER TWO

THE LONDON HOUSEHOLD settled down quickly to its ordinary afternoon routine. There were occasional murmurings of wonder and disbelief but these soon faded as a hush of quiet expectancy settled upon the rooms. The tiptoeing of servants, the muted voices and the drained expressions might have given a visitor unacquainted with the family the erroneous impression that someone had just passed away.

The lady of the house, emptied of all emotion, retrieved the once neglected letter from the floor to be read over and over.

There was no misconstruing the message it contained, no matter how desperately she tried. Sir Antony did not consider himself worthy of her; he was attempting to be gallant.

Lizzie returned to the window seat and let the last dying rays of the afternoon sun warm her neck and shoulders. She had fallen in love with Sir Antony Russelford the moment they had met. She remembered it all so well.

It was springtime, as it was now, and Reggie, down from school, had brought home a friend. The boys were fifteen or sixteen, which meant that she had been no more than ten or eleven, although that could hardly signify in how she felt. Tony was tall, taller than Reggie—but that had changed—and so handsome! A pair of startling blue eyes stared at her from under an unruly mop of brown hair. His eyes were so blue and they smiled at her. He was shy but she had known then, with the same conviction she now felt, that Antony Russelford was the man she would marry.

Seven terrified years were spent wondering and waiting. What if by the time she were old enough, he had found someone else and—it was too horrible to imagine—had married? Each birthday passed with interminable slowness until her coming out.

The fifth Earl of Drenview, however, thwarted his daughter's plans by choosing a most inopportune time to depart this world. That, at least, was the opinion of his youngest child, for it meant a year wasted in mourning.

A word must be said at this point in poor Lizzie's defense. She was always the most dutiful of children and, in fact, loved her father dearly, but as was his death, so was his life. Robert Croyton had an innate ability to be a source of pain for his children. It was not that he was cruel; it was quite simply a case of not being there when he was needed and always being there when he was—most emphatically—not wanted. So perhaps it is fitting that the peer should have left his life in the same manner in which he lived it—inconveniently.

The year of mourning passed and it had not been without its advantages. The two men continued their friendship into manhood. Tony had seen a great deal of Reggie and, therefore, Elizabeth. But when Sir Geoffrey Russelford fell victim to a prolonged brain fever, his only son was thrust into the imbroglio of managing a too-long-mismanaged estate. Sir Antony was overwhelmed by the vastness of his task, and Lizzie could only imagine how painful it must have been—must still be—for him. Lizzie was forthright, to a fault some would say, and Sir

Antony's shyness was something she had never fully understood. It made him appeal to her, struck a responsive chord within her, but she was often frustrated by it.

The last time she had seen him, he had stood in this very room staring into the fireplace, unable to face her. Ostensibly, he had called to see Reggie but the earl was out and he stayed to explain the reason for his departure. His father's interests in Jamaica were his only salvation. He was going personally to see to them, with every hope of salvaging the estate, but he had no idea when or if he would return. Lizzie said she understood; yet she would have married him then and gone with him if only he had asked. He hadn't. Sir Antony would ask nothing of her; he didn't expect her to return his feelings, but he simply had to tell her how he felt. He would not presume, he said.

Just as he would not presume now, she thought as she reviewed the letter.

The Toast of British society had waited nonetheless. Denying suitor after suitor, the Beauty survived almost three long years of incessant advances by moon-eyed youths. She kept busy deliberately and never stopped long enough to consider her situation. Reckless abandon and a zest for all things new and exciting were shields Lizzie displayed to the world. Spurred on by nothing more than a hope she never permitted herself to wonder what would happen if Sir Antony didn't return. That possibility was unthinkable.

As involved as her mind was with these matters, Lizzie did not ignore her commitment to attend the soirée given by Lord and Lady Graneville that evening. It was with some absentmindedness that she prepared for the affair and not until she arrived at the steps of the good couple's home did she fully emerge from her reverie.

The party was, as expected, marvellously attended, for few people fortunate enough to be invited would fail to put in an appearance.

"Why, Lizzie, my dear," said her inimitable hostess in greeting, "where is that charming brother of yours? He promised me he would come."

Lizzie smiled charmingly herself. "He sends his regrets, Aunt Martie. He was unavoidably called away on business."

"Business? Reggie? What can the world be coming to?" Lady Graneville laughed heartily.

A dear friend of the family since before Lizzie could remember, Lady Graneville was a stout woman of uncertain age but with a keen eye. This eye she now trained upon Lizzie as if she were examining a specimen of unknown origin.

Lizzie looked exceedingly lovely as she was wont to do when she least tried. A gown of blue crepe moulded itself to her figure with beguiling ease, and the rustle of her petticoats indicated fine silk. A cream-coloured cambric shawl was draped artlessly about arms clothed in long gloves of a similiar material and golden ringlets framed an equally creamy complexion like a halo.

No fault could be found with the younger lady's appearance. The quick glance did not fail, however, to detect the worried look in her eyes or the slight frown. Lady Graneville could not help but feel concerned and resolved to keep her eye upon Elizabeth Croyton.

There was neither censure nor approbation in this resolve. She had no children of her own, so it was perhaps natural that all the maternal instincts of the good lady should have been redirected to the children of her best friend. Because they had lost their mother at a very tender age, and there being no other female relative suitable to attend to their upbringing, Lady Graneville had taken this great task upon herself. The chore was made ever more taxing by the abrupt nature of the late earl. He was very much opposed to what he termed "that woman's infernal interference." But while he muttered this in the company of his friends, he did little to involve himself in his children's lives, and permitted Lady Graneville a free rein.

The next hour passed quickly as Lizzie danced and chatted with her more persistent swains. As soon as was possible, she broke free to walk arm in arm with her best friend, Miss Valerie Bach.

The two young women, inseparable since school, left no topic untouched. Valerie alone knew her friend's secrets and, without qualm or reservation, Lizzie divulged the latest events.

"Oh, Lizzie," her friend exclaimed, "how wonderful that he's coming home!"

"Yes," she agreed, "I have missed him so, and I've been frightfully worried that something terrible might befall him."

"Indeed, I hadn't noticed," Valerie replied breezily and with a soft giggle. "Only that you speak of no one save Sir Antony Russelford."

"Oh, my dearest Val, have I neglected you?"

"No," replied Miss Bach honestly. "Papa says I should be honoured that you condescend to associate beneath your class."

"Valerie! What nonsense!"

"For you, perhaps, but not to Papa. And Mama worries that I shall never catch a husband if I'm forever in your company, for no man could notice me compared to you." The sorrowful voice brightened as she added ingenuously, "I haven't been brave enough to tell her that

I meet far more gentlemen because of you than I should ever meet without you."

Undoubtedly, Valerie Bach was overshadowed by her friend's more striking beauty. But, unimpressed by her own appearance, Lizzie considered Valerie's soft brown ringlets far more appealing than her own improbably bright curls. It was an unlikely camaraderie to most eyes as Valerie Bach was shy and demure whilst Lizzie oppositely inclined in nature; yet Valerie possessed the singular ability to be a comfort to her troubled companion. Simply to be in her company was a soothing balm upon Lizzie's restless spirit and provided a confidante both understanding and devout. Valerie, on the other hand, was attracted to Lizzie's frank and friendly openness, living vicariously through her friend's exciting exploits and revelling in the occasions when she discovered herself drawn into them. Adventure was not foreseeable in her life, although recently events had taken a decided turn for the better.

She was in love with Martin Costain, son of Sir Rodney Costain, baronet. "Is he not the most handsome of men, Lizzie?" She extolled the virtues of her adored longingly.

The two girls strolled to a quiet corner of the room and thereby allowed themselves an unimpaired view of the proceedings. The object of their conversation danced by them expertly with one of Miss Bach's sisters. He was a florid youth a year younger than Lord Croyton but with an equally assured air, and his features appeared sculpted in their dark fineness.

"Yes, he's quite handsome," agreed Lizzie as she quelled the shudder of apprehension running down her spine. There was an indefinite quality about Martin Costain which she could not like. His manners were most pleasing—almost too pleasing—and there was a devilry in the way he curled his lip sardonically whenever he spoke. Lizzie was wiser than to put words to her feelings in the presence of Valerie. To criticize would be to wound her friend and she had no desire to do so.

"I know Mama doesn't approve," the girl continued, unperturbed by Lizzie's reticence. "But I'm certain Papa won't object. There are five of us and one can't expect him to keep us all under his roof, no matter how much he says he'd miss us. And think of the attachment—a baronet's son! Oh, I know it's nothing to you, but to Papa that's very important, no matter how much money he has. I know Mama feels the same way although she doesn't like to show it. To marry her daughters off to Quality—that would be quite a triumph."

"Are you thinking of marriage?" Lizzie could not erase the note of surprise from her voice.

"I really shouldn't say this," confessed Valerie with a giggle. "I'll probably jinx myself, but I shouldn't be surprised if Mr. Costain speaks to Papa very soon."

"Why, Val! I had no idea it was so serious."

"Oh, yes. Now I know you wouldn't say anything. I should be devastated if he didn't," she admitted, and the sudden envisaging of this catastrophe brought a tear to her eye.

Lizzie rose to the occasion with reassurances. "Oh, my dear, you mustn't take on so," she said. "I'm sure everything will work out just the way you want. But tell me, what makes you think he will propose? Has he said anything to you?"

"He doesn't need to say anything," insisted Miss Bach righteously. "He's been the most perfect gentleman. It's just...oh, Lizzie...You're so beautiful. Men must always be asking for your hand. You could have your pick of husbands. I . . . I'm not that lucky. Mr. Costain's the first man who has even paid the slightest attention to me even for all Papa's money. That has to count for something, doesn't it?''

Unable to ignore her friend's imploring eyes, Lizzie patted the other girl's hand absently. "I'm certain it does," she said and kept any opinion of what exactly accounted for this unsolicited attention discreetly to herself.

The news disturbed her. Where had she been not to notice the infatuation? And why did Valerie wait until now to mention it? They had been without secrets since the day of their meeting, with their heads locked together in hushed confidences and hesitant giggles all through their schooling.

Lizzie broke from her thoughts at the sudden appearance at her side of Martin Costain. "I'm terrible sorry, sir, I didn't hear what you said. I'm afraid I was daydreaming."

Dark brown eyes gleamed appreciatively at her confusion. "That's quite all right," he replied. "I was merely sayin' the usual pleasantries which, like as not, deserve to be ignored."

His voice possessed a low singsong quality with the faintest of accents hinting at an Irish connection.

"I was merely sayin' that I don't see your brother," repeated Mr. Costain with a boyishly irresistible quality to his smile. "I trust he's well?"

"Yes, he's quite well."

"I'm surprised I don't see him here." He surveyed the room briefly. "As I recall he was always one for bashes on the grand scale."

"My brother has business in Bristol," Lizzie answered and recalled the reason for his departure with a slight pang of guilt. "He would certainly have come to-night otherwise."

Mr. Costain appeared unaccountably pleased and probed further. "Away for long?" he asked.

"Oh, no, he should return in a day or two." The lie rose swiftly to her lips. She was in no danger, but a feeling of general uneasiness seized her, and she racked her brain in search of a different topic of conversation.

"Valerie was telling me, sir, that you have just returned from a trip of your own," she said with a smile. "The Continent, I believe?"

"Yes, just a short tour of France," Mr. Costain replied dismissively. "Nothing dramatic, of course. I've been there several times before. I find it healthful to escape the drudgery of this confining little island every now and again."

The sardonic curl of his upper lip belied the whimsical air with which he spoke. It was obvious to all but the uninitiated that there were particular reasons why Mr. Costain found it healthful to leave England upon occasion.

Valerie was hopelessly uninitiated. "It can be so dreary here at times, especially in the winter," she said. "I understand Italy is the place to go in the winter. Have you been there, Mr. Costain?"

"Several times, and it's very beautiful. Particularly Venice—it is the city of lovers, y'know."

He took no obvious notice of the embarrassed confusion he had caused and added artlessly, "But actually I prefer Spain to Italy. The Spaniards are a simpler people and more innocent, but there's charm in simplicity and innocence, don't you agree, Miss Bach?"

Valerie's eyes remained lowered but her cheeks gave evidence of the strength of her feelings.

Lizzie stepped in to cover her friend's discomfiture and said swiftly, "I think, sir, that that would depend upon your definition of simplicity and innocence. If by 'simplicity,' you mean their lives are less complicated by material objects—is there not also more hardship, more suffering? And, if in their 'innocence' they ignore the causes and do not strive to overcome them, then are they not more hurt? Where is the charm, sir?"

"Faith, you've taught me a lesson. I shall have to be more careful with my opinions in future. I thank you." He laughed and bowed grandly before turning to Valerie. "I wonder, Miss Bach, if you would be so kind as to give me the honour of this next dance?"

"Oh, yes. Certainly."

Relief shone in Valerie's eyes. She would not have been human if she had not experienced a momentary doubt in her lover's steadfastness upon meeting the inimitable Beauty. Lizzie would never deliberately steal him away, knowing how she felt, but men were such silly creatures—her mother had taught her that. They were more likely to fall in love with a beautiful face than what lay behind it. This was not to cast any aspersions upon Lizzie, who was quite intelligent indeed as well as being the sweetest friend she had ever had; it was simply a fact of life.

Lady Elizabeth had admirers enough, for no less than three gentlemen descended upon her the moment Costain escorted Valerie to the floor. Like bees to the proverbial flower, they hovered and buzzed; yet this flower was not without defences. Smiling demurely, she refused them all in turn and sent them away unabashedly in search of sweeter—by that is meant more accessible — nectar.

Lizzie searched for someone else in the crowd, and it was a moment before she spotted her target.

Lady Graneville was notorious for planting herself in a chair and remaining there for an entire evening. Considering her remarkable girth, this tendency was understandable, but it did nothing to diminish her command of any situation. Her signals were so finely tuned that a slight movement of a finger was enough to cause a glass of champagne or a dessert to appear at her elbow. There was no magic in this, only the unquestioning attendance of his lordship and a bevy of faithful servants.

As quickly as possible, Lizzie broached the subject uppermost in her mind. "Tell me, Aunt Martie, what do you know of Martin Costain?"

An expression of disapproval settled upon the lady's expansive features. "I made a terrible mistake in allowing Mr. Naper to bring a friend," complained Lady Graneville. "If I had known it was to be That Man, I would never have done so. I wasn't aware you knew him, my dear. I do not approve."

"Miss Bach knows him quite well."

"I knew nothing good could come of your association with that girl," she sniffed.

"Valerie is quite kind and sweet. I don't think she has any idea of his . . . his reputation."

Lady Graneville gave her adopted niece a keen stare. "And what do you know of his 'reputation,' my dear?"

"Only what I've heard from Reggie."

"I shall have a word with your brother when he returns," she muttered. "Imagine. Speaking of such things to his own sister! What else has he told you which he shouldn't have?"

Lizzie blushed at the memory of that afternoon's conversation regarding Mr. Forbisher but wisely refrained from mentioning it and strove instead to defend her poor maligned sibling.

"He didn't tell me anything," she replied. "It's just little things that, well, set one to thinking. I mean...I've heard the same elsewhere...well, perhaps not quite the same, Reggie does tell a good story when the mood strikes him. Oh, dear, Aunt Martie, you can't blame Reggie. It's not his fault that I can wheedle things out of him."

The appeal on her brother's behalf was lame at best but appeased the older woman.

"No, I suppose one can't blame Reggie," she admitted. "The poor boy has no sense. But mark my words, girl, I shall speak to him. Where did you say he was gone to?"

"Bristol."

"Harrumph. Just like the young to go galavanting about the countryside for no apparent reason."

The fact that this judgement was diametrically opposed to Lord Croyton's languid character was lost on the two ladies.

"Aunt Martie, you haven't answered my question," Lizzie prompted. "What can you tell me about Martin Costain? It's rather important."

"Stay away from him. The man has no scruples and he would be the first to tell you so. It's that Irish blood, I'm certain. His father, Sir Rodney, has the best of manners and is quite the gentleman but he took up with That Woman and that was his downfall. Oh, she was a beauty—just the type to catch a man's fancy—but there was a devilry about her, just as there's a devilry about her son.

"If Martin Costain has attached himself in any manner to your friend, then it can only be for one reason—

money. I shudder to think what will happen when Sir Rodney finally passes on. That huge fortune will be squandered most dreadfully. Young Costain is always tight for money, I understand, and he gets a sizeable allowance. It's shocking, that's what it is.

"If this girl is as sweet as you say," ruminated Lady Graneville, "then it could be that she truly doesn't understand. I shouldn't be surprised, considering her mother. That woman can't see past the end of her nose—most disagreeable. She actually thinks her daughters can do no wrong! And one of them is associating with the Costain cub—la, what a tale!"

"Aunt Martie! You can't! Valerie Bach is my friend!"

"In that case," she pronounced with a firm nod, "you would be wise to warn her off of him—if you can."

The subject was closed as Lady Graneville turned her attention to the glass of champagne which had magically appeared at her side.

Lizzie cogitated upon the information received. Martin Costain might be the son of a baronet and the heir to a sizeable fortune, but he had managed at a young age to acquire quite a reputation, and not a good one. The telling of his story was not meant for tender ears and Lizzie was aware of no more than the more pallid details of his checkered past, having gleaned these from her brother's conversations. Lady Graneville had merely confirmed what she already knew. Mr. Costain expertly depleted himself of his allowance on a regular basis and always in the most diverting fashion—at least to himself and his hangers-on.

His manners, similar to those of all who lived by their wits, were finely honed and definitely pleasing. He was especially enjoyed by the older ladies, in whose presence a young rake ready with a ribald comment or lascivious leer was always welcome. And Mr. Costain possessed an air of innocent, boyish charm which added immeasurably to the fun. He preferred the risky gamble—the more risk or the higher the stakes the better.

All these thoughts flashed through Lizzie's mind as she observed the look of rapture upon her dancing friend's face. She would keep a close watch on the relationship, for she was not going to see Valerie hurt. She set aside her own problems as her mind raced with possible outcomes to the romance unfolding before her. Unless there was a drastic and totally unexpected character change in Mr. Costain, the possibility of which she doubted, the future did indeed look dismal.

Lady Elizabeth, however, was not the only person concerned by Martin Costain's attentions to the elder Miss Bach. A portly gentleman watched the couple from the opposite wall and his brow furrowed in an unpleasant frown.

CHAPTER THREE

THE SUN SHONE brightly into the library and Lizzie curled up on the window seat with the latest romance. The heroine was a miserable creature, the plot pathetically silly and her attention wandered correspondingly.

Childers entered. "Pardon me, my lady. A gentleman caller."

Lizzie accepted the proffered card. "For me?" She asked.

"He requested to see you specifically. I have shown him into the small parlour." There was no hint of stricture in Childers's tone but the small parlour was never used for more welcome guests.

Her curiosity aroused, Lizzie wasted no time in greeting her visitor. She was disappointed at first glance.

The gentleman was small in stature but not likely to remain so in girth for many more years. This propensity manifested itself in a straining waistcoat and massive jowls. Lizzie wondered if the redness of his face was a natural condition or due to the tightness of his clothes. His attire was conservative and, although not of the latest style, fashionable and he had obviously taken care in dressing for this meeting. The dark brown frock coat, tan waistcoat, milky breeches and modishly tied cravat all bespoke a man of simple means, a man of business or a gentleman in reduced circumstances.

Aside from the beet colour of his face, the only feature worth remarking upon were his eyes. They were the palest blue Lizzie had ever encountered and, magnified by the spectacles perched upon his nose, flitted nervously about.

She smiled coolly. "How do you do, Mr. Wallace? I don't believe I've had the pleasure of making your acquaintance. Are you perhaps a friend of my brother's?"

Mr. Wallace bowed slightly over her hand. "Ah, no, Lady Elizabeth, I have not had the pleasure of meeting his lordship. And I would not have come today if I had not thought it important. I apologize for any intrusion."

"You will forgive me then if I do not understand what we can possibly have to discuss of such importance."

Her guest's hands fluttered. "A mutual friend, Lady Elizabeth," he explained. "Miss Valerie Bach."

"I do not discuss my friends with strangers, Mr. Wallace," she said, bridling. "You would be wise to do the same."

"Please believe me," burst out Mr. Wallace, "I have the highest regard for Miss Bach. Indeed, I...I love her." The announcement seemed to unleash a tidal wave of emotion in the man. "I love her so deeply that it pains me," he said.

He wrung his hands helplessly and paced. "Perhaps I was wrong to come here, but...but I saw you last night speaking to her and I knew you were friends. She speaks very highly of you. I felt I had to do something, that...that if she would listen to anyone it must be you."

"Did you wish me to speak to her on your behalf?"

"No!" Panic rose in his voice. "No...no, of course not. She barely knows I exist." He laughed dismally. "I...I'm not the bravest of men, you see. I haven't spoken to her of my feelings. To her, I'm afraid I shall always be just an acquaintance, and a minor one. Besides, I'm very much afraid I could not compete. I haven't the address nor the . . . the appearance.''

Lizzie was forced to acknowledge to herself that such was indeed the case, but the evident strength of the poor gentleman's feelings softened her.

"Please be seated, Mr. Wallace—" she indicated a chair "—and continue."

Mr. Wallace seated himself with no mishap—much to Lizzie's amazement—and she studied him carefully. "I am extremely fond of Miss Bach, sir,'' she began. "She has been a friend since we were in school together. She is kind and sweet and perhaps the most innocent person I know. I would not wish to see her hurt in any manner. And although I can sympathize with your feelings, I fail to see how I can be of help to you."

"It is not me I wish you to help, Lady Elizabeth. I am very well aware of my failings . . . my inadequacies. Only God can help me with those.

"It is Miss Bach I wish you to help. I am very much afraid for her well-being. It is a delicate matter, which is why I have waited until now to approach you. I had hoped the matter would pass and now I think I may have delayed too long. . . .''

Lizzie waved his ramblings aside. "To what matter are you referring exactly, Mr. Wallace?"

"Martin Costain."

Mr. Wallace was subjected to a cold hard stare which did nothing to increase his confidence. His hand rose unconsciously to his tie and his face grew a shade redder, however impossible that might have seemed.

"I . . . I mean no disrespect to Miss Bach—" he groped for words "—but . . . but the association . . ." His tie grew ever tighter.

"I understand, Mr. Wallace. I cannot like it, either."

A sigh of relief escaped his lips. "Then you will speak to her?"

Lizzie shook her head. "What could I say? I would only offend her."

"But—"

"If anyone should speak to her, it should be you, sir. Oh, not about Martin Costain, of course, but about yourself—your feelings. I feel certain if she knew their depth—"

"I couldn't," said the young man in a panic. "You don't understand. I have nothing. I receive only a modest income—extremely modest. I could hardly afford the style of life to which she is accustomed. And I would wish to do so on my own. I work for my uncle, you see, in Bath. The only reason I came to London at all was on his behalf. He has business with Miss Bach's father. That's how I met her. I've managed to find one reason and another to stay on, but I cannot do so indefinitely. I must return soon.

"Besides, her father would never approve of the match. My uncle has six children—all boys, all healthy—so I shall receive nothing on that count. He would think me after her money." He sighed deeply. "Frankly, I can understand how he might think so. So you see, that is why I came to you. Certainly, there is *something* you can do."

"You may think your feelings do you justice, Mr. Wallace, but I find your reasons demeaning," snapped Lizzie with far more vehemence than she had intended. She gained control of herself, seeing the shock on the other's face.

"I apologize if I've sounded overly harsh. I am myself a wealthy woman and I know I would feel insulted if

I learned that ... that a man had denied his true feelings for me simply because of ... of what he thought others might say, or to appease his own vanity. Give us women more credit for knowing our own feelings, sir."

The silence that fell between them lasted so long that Mr. Wallace's uneasiness manifested itself in several tugs at his waistcoat. He was on the verge of speaking when Lizzie broke the stillness brusquely.

"Perhaps there is something I can do, Mr. Wallace," she said, capitulating, "but I will require your assistance."

"Anything," came the fervent reply.

"Good. I wonder if you would be available later this afternoon for a ride in Hyde Park, say about three?"

"Ah, yes. I should have to borrow a horse."

"Do so. Miss Bach and I will be riding together in my curricle. You will have no trouble spotting us."

"What are you proposing to do?"

"We shall distract Miss Bach from Mr. Costain and allow the two of you to become better acquainted. I am a very swift judge of character, Mr. Wallace, and I was not the least impressed by Mr. Costain's. I do, however, like you. You have a friend and an ally."

"Thank you, thank you." Mr. Wallace's smile disappeared almost as quickly as it came. "I don't think you'll have much luck though—" he rose slowly and with effort "—considering."

"You must have more courage, Mr. Wallace, and more faith in Miss Bach."

"Yes, yes, of course," he replied, shamefaced. "I'm sorry I could have thought it. It's only that I've been so distressed of late ..."

"It's quite all right. I understand." She held out her hand and concluded, "I have tremendous faith in Miss

Bach and no faith in Martin Costain. We must distract them both if our plan is to work. Never fear, I think I know just the way.''

When the distraught gentleman finally took his leave, Lizzie was immediately amazed at how Providence stepped in at precisely the right moment. The depth and honesty of Mr. Wallace's feelings should be enough to lure Valerie's attentions away from Martin Costain but Lizzie doubted they would. Mr. Wallace was quite correct. He did not possess the presence to compete with one of Costain's ilk.

There might be a way, however, of distracting Martin Costain from Valerie. It was not a pleasant alternative and Lizzie ran the risk of losing a friend forever, but it was a chance she felt was worth taking.

THE RISK presented itself sooner than anticipated as the afternoon sun radiated upon the park, hidden by an occasional fluffy white cloud. What breeze existed disturbed only the lightest of green leaves.

It could not have been a lovelier scene, Lizzie thought as Valerie chatted gaily beside her. Her topic of conversation, however, left much to be desired, centring as it did upon Mr. Costain, and Lizzie searched the park expectantly for Mr. Wallace.

''Val, darling—'' she interrupted her friend ''—why didn't you tell me sooner about your feelings for Mr. Costain?''

''Frankly, Lizzie, I didn't think you would approve,'' admitted Valerie. ''I can see I was only being missish. You do like him, don't you?''

Lizzie pretended involvement with handling the horses and when she turned to Valerie's smiling face, her eye fortuitously caught a glimpse of Mr. Wallace.

Unfortunately, the gentleman looked most uncomfortable upon his mount. The horse was quite fresh and strenuously insistent upon having its own head and it required all Mr. Wallace's expertise to keep the animal on a relatively straight course. He managed somehow and pulled alongside the curricle just as Lizzie reined her own team to a halt.

"Why, Mr. Wallace, what a pleasant surprise!" she exclaimed and smiled brightly, more in an attempt to hide her own amusement than from any genuine pleasure. "You know Miss Bach, I'm certain?"

"Yes, yes. How do you do, ladies?" He bowed slightly from the saddle and almost landed upon the ground for his efforts, as his mount chose that particular moment to do a most graceful sidestep. By the time he mastered the animal, both women had concealed their mirth.

"I don't believe I've ever seen you here before, Mr. Wallace," Valerie remarked politely.

"Ah, no. I don't get out much, but today was so beautiful, I couldn't resist."

"It is lovely weather," she agreed and looked beseechingly to Lizzie, who seemed unusually absorbed in what was happening at the other end of the park. Wondering at her friend's extraordinary rudeness, Valerie asked, "Do you ride often, Mr. Wallace?"

In answer, his horse did a precision pirouette entirely of its own volition. Sheer instinct for self-preservation kept Mr. Wallace in the saddle and his face took on an awful shade of purple as he breathed heavily. "Ah, actually, no. To be honest this is the first time I've ever been on a horse. I don't think I'm doing very well. Do you ride?"

"Oh, yes. I enjoy riding immensely."

"Oh."

Valerie glanced at his dismayed expression timidly. "Might I make a small suggestion?" She ventured. "You do look so uncomfortable."

"I'm never one to ignore advice from an expert," he responded.

"Well, I wouldn't say I'm an expert," she declaimed sweetly. "It's only that I've found when riding a horse I don't know very well that it's best to try to be as relaxed as possible. I don't know how, but they seem to be able to sense when you're particularly nervous or don't know what you're doing."

"Relax." He took a deep breath and exhaled slowly. "A capital idea. I feel better already, Miss Bach. Thank you, I shall try to remember."

"You're welcome, sir."

Mr. Wallace took a second deep breath, only to have it end in a gulp as the equine miscreant executed another dance step. "I shall also have to remember not to relax *too* much," he added.

Valerie looked down at her lap to hide her smile.

"Faith, and now I see why the sun is hiding behind a cloud—two such beautiful ladies in one carriage—it can't compete. Miss Bach...Lady Elizabeth." Martin Costain bowed gallantly from horseback as his gaze fell upon Mr. Wallace. "I don't believe I've had the pleasure, sir," he remarked.

Lizzie frowned but completed the introductions with dispatch, and while the two men scrutinized each other closely, she noticed with dismay how quickly Valerie perked up. Her face was alive with interest, all directed toward the new arrival.

Costain was the first to return his attention to the ladies, for a cursory glance was enough to convince him that Mr. Wallace posed no threat.

"Ah, there's the sun!" He exclaimed. "Miss Bach smiles."

Valerie giggled as Lizzie mentally condemned the ridiculous prosing. "What a pleasure to see you again, Mr. Costain." She smiled brightly to the gentleman at her side. "It is a lovely day, isn't it? What more could Miss Bach and I ask for? In the company of two such charming gentlemen?"

Valerie blinked at the abrupt change in her friend.

"I don't know. What could you ask for?" Costain returned cautiously.

"Why, sir, only that the day should never end." She laughed gaily.

Martin Costain's smile grew wider and his eyes twinkled down into hers. "I cannot speak for Mr. Wallace," he professed, "but if it were in my power, I should grant your wish."

"Oh, but sir, it is not in your power." She pouted and glanced up at him from under her lashes and asked coyly, "Or is it?"

Mr. Wallace observed the outrageous display of flirtation with almost as shocked an expression as Valerie's. He saw the look of anguish in her eyes and immediately attracted her attention.

"I happened to notice you at Assembly last night, Miss Bach. Did you enjoy it?"

Valerie tore her eyes away from Lizzie and Costain with reluctance. "Oh, yes...yes, I did," she murmured. "Thank you. I do so enjoy dancing. Do you, Mr. Wallace?"

"Yes, I do enjoy it. Although I cannot say I've had much opportunity of late—being here on business."

"Oh, yes, you're from Bath. Do you drink the waters?"

Lizzie's playful laugh caught her ear and she wondered what they could be talking about to make Martin smile so.

"No, I don't drink the waters," answered Mr. Wallace. "I have tried it, but quite frankly it tastes vile. Miss Bach?"

The girl's wounded expression caused Mr. Wallace to release his grip upon the reins. He realized his mistake too late as the horse shied backward, reared and deposited him on the hard ground with bone-jarring abruptness.

"Oh, my goodness!" Valerie cried.

Mr. Wallace sat up to discover all eyes upon him.

"Are you unhurt?" Lizzie asked.

"Yes, yes, I'm fine. Thank you."

His former mount nudged his shoulder playfully and he grabbed the reins and slowly heaved himself to a standing position.

"After all this," he said with a laugh, "now he likes me." He smiled goodnaturedly and bowed. "For my next trick, I shall *walk* home."

"They say," Costain offered, "that it's best to get right back on."

"I'm certain that is the best thing to do, sir," agreed Mr. Wallace, "but you will forgive me if I feel I have offered enough entertainment for one afternoon." He made his leg to the ladies and dejectedly led his horse away.

Lizzie watched him go guiltily. The ride in the park had been her idea and it had ended so miserably. Why hadn't he told her he couldn't ride?

"Interesting fellow," Costain remarked with a sly grin.

"Yes," Valerie agreed quietly, remembering his sad eyes just before the fall.

"I think Miss Bach and I should take our example from him." Lizzie gathered up the reins. "The afternoon is getting on, sir. You will excuse us."

Costain had barely time to make his bow before Lizzie whipped the horses into step.

It was some moments before either girl spoke.

"Your Mr. Wallace is very agreeable, Lizzie," Valerie ventured.

"*My* Mr. Wallace?" asked Lizzie with a laugh. "Oh, Val, you say the most wonderful things sometimes. I'm not the least bit interested in Dexter Wallace. You, of all people, should know that. I already told you, he's a friend of Reggie's."

"Oh." Valerie examined her friend closely. "I'm happy you like Martin," she said. "I was afraid at first that you didn't."

Lizzie manoeuvred the curricle out of the park with ease.

"I would have hated that to happen," the girl continued. "I would miss having you for a friend."

"You'll always have me as a friend, Val. Have you been reading those terrible novels again?" Lizzie tried to sound as breezy as possible and demanded, "Now, let's discuss something else. I saw the most marvellous hat at Mrs. Trentley's the other day. I thought it would be just the thing for you."

CHAPTER FOUR

THE NEXT WEEK passed in such a flurry of activity that Lizzie could barely recall its events. Parties, routs and Assemblies whizzed about her, and throughout the whole she strove to present Mr. Wallace in the best possible light. She made certain he was always available and that Valerie spent considerable time with him. To do so she found herself in the awkward position of spending more time with Martin Costain.

The strategy was succeeding but taking a considerable toll upon her mental resources. She was extremely tired and had no time to consider her own problems.

These were brought home to her with complete abruptness as she prepared to join her good friend for a riding expedition. She skipped down the entry hall stairs and stopped in middescent at the presence of a large gentleman entering from the street.

"Tony!"

The two years and more had moulded Sir Antony Russelford significantly. He left a gawky, if handsome, youth and returned a man with a tall, straight and well-muscled frame and—as the removal of his greatcoat testified—a pair of wide, strong shoulders. His youthful features which Lizzie remembered so well, were more chiselled, and had it not been for the shy blue eyes gazing up at her, she might have found recognition difficult. The vaguest hint of a smile haunted his thin lips.

"Lizzie," said Sir Antony, motioning to her riding habit, "if I had known you were going to be out, I wouldn't have bothered to come. I don't wish to intrude upon your plans."

"Nonsense." Lizzie bounded down the remainder of the stairs and insisted, "Of course it's no intrusion."

"You're even more beautiful than I remembered!" he exclaimed with a laugh as her outstretched hands slipped snugly into his.

Her cheeks warmed under his ardent gaze and, momentarily flustered at the discovery that she could indeed blush, Lizzie glanced behind him quickly. "Did you just arrive?" she asked. "Where's Reggie?"

"I have no idea where your brother is," admitted a slightly puzzled Sir Antony. "I haven't seen him in almost three years and I didn't come to see him now."

"He didn't meet you?"

"Meet me? No, no one met me. I came into London last night and you're the first person I've seen." He frowned and his voice grew hesitant. "I wanted to speak to you. You received my letter?"

At the reference, Lizzie lost her smile. She disengaged her hands and turned. "We can speak in the library," she said brusquely.

"We received your letter last week," she replied as the door closed behind Sir Antony. "Reggie left for Bristol to meet your ship, but it seems he could not even do that right."

"Pray don't blame Reggie." He smiled apologetically. "My ship had a run of good weather and put into port ahead of schedule. I left for London without delay." His brow furrowed as he asked, "Why would Reggie come to meet me? He must have known I would come here immediately."

Lizzie waved her hand uselessly and left his question unanswered. She strode to a window with no idea how to respond, but her indecision proved unnecessary.

Sir Antony answered his own question. "It was because of my letter, wasn't it? I thought if I wrote, it might prepare—"

"How very considerate of you to be so concerned for our feelings!" Lizzie spun about and her eyes flashed all the pain she had stored since receiving his message. "Especially considering how all your letters were lies from the start. Did you think we might not want to know the truth of how things were faring with you? What hurts is that you could not trust us enough to be honest."

Sir Antony spread out his hands and shrugged. "I'm sorry if I hurt you. Believe me, I didn't intend it. It's merely that things went so poorly I didn't wish to worry you. I see I was wrong. I realized that when I wrote to you. I also realized my position in regard to other matters."

His energy released itself in pacing. "I am an extremely poor man," he explained. "If I have a hundred pounds to my name, I should be very much surprised. It would be wrong of me to...to presume upon your feelings. I can offer you nothing."

"Do you think that I should care for such? I am in a position where it does not matter."

"*I* care, and it matters very deeply to me. Lizzie, I said some things before I left which I had no right to say or to even think. I cannot apologize for them; neither can I ask you to forgive me."

"But you wish to recant them nonetheless," Lizzie murmured desolately with the hot sting of tears behind her eyes. "Have your feelings changed so, sir?"

"My situation has changed," replied the baronet evasively. "It's hard to put into words to make you understand—call it male pride, if you will."

"I would call it something else," she flung at him. "You made a promise."

"I made no promises," he returned sharply, his jaw clenched firm. "It all depended upon my situation—you knew that before I left. I never asked you to wait."

"But you knew I would," she argued madly. "And your letters never hinted otherwise—until now." She waved her hand again and banished the issue. "Can't you see that you're just being unreasonably old-fashioned and silly? Reggie cannot possibly have any objections, if I don't."

"I would not even bring the matter up to him," he said flatly.

Lizzie recognized the tone. She had never before encountered this unyielding stubbornness in Sir Antony, but she remembered the quality in her father. The matter was finished; his decision would not be changed. She stood for several moments, uncomprehending, before smiling faintly.

"Oh, Tony, let's not argue," she pleaded. "What a terrible homecoming—to argue so. I don't remember us ever having words before. Isn't it silly?

"You've changed a little," she said judiciously as she took a step toward him and searched his impassive features for some hint of his former self.

"Too much has happened to me, Lizzie," he replied quietly. "Too much, too soon, to even begin to explain. I shouldn't have come."

"Now you truly are being silly. Not to call would be the most horrid thing to do. Whatever would Reggie say? He sets great faith in you.

"We've . . . I've missed you."

"I've missed you, too."

A small awkward silence descended between them until Sir Antony cleared his throat and cocked an eyebrow. "Has it been so long that we're reduced to speaking platitudes?"

"Oh, Tony," she answered with a small choking laugh, "I thought it should be so wonderful when you finally returned and I cannot even think now that you are here. I am the most perfect goose."

"The most perfectly beautiful goose," he agreed.

A surer giggle greeted him and Sir Antony recognized her mood restored, for in the next instant, Lizzie wiped her eyes, swept him to a chair and commanded, "Sit down, Tony, and you must tell me everything. Do not dare to omit a single detail."

"I shouldn't know where to begin," he said with a shrug, but under Lizzie's warm and watchful gaze soon had described in a few terse words what his letters failed to express—his intense disappointment at discovering that his father's "grand plantation" consisted of five tumbledown shanties overgrown by tropical vegetation. Educated but untrained and possessing no skills other than a command of Latin and a determination stemming from desperation, Sir Antony had hacked, toiled and sweated to bring the land to production. His trials only served to reinforce in his quick mind how illprepared he was to assume such awesome responsibility.

Her attention now devoted entirely to the baronet, Lizzie perceived minute changes in his manner and appearance. The deep resonating tones of his voice were no longer timorous but immensely weary. Tiny, faint lines accented his lips and drew them downward. He was calmer, sober, less withdrawn yet somehow less alive than she remembered. Her eyes alighted upon the large hands resting comfortably upon his upraised knee. They were scarred, calloused and unnaturally quiet. Only then did she recognize what strain the past two years had wreaked upon him, and she condemned her selfishness for not noticing immediately.

"Why did you not tell me sooner?" she asked softly.

"It is not your problem," responded Sir Antony.

She blinked at the judgement. "If it is not, sir, pray tell me what is?"

He leaned forward, interlaced his fingers and, acknowledging her point, smiled wanly. "What help could you have given?" he queried.

"I? None," she admitted honestly, "but I am not without resources and I do possess an elder brother whom you forget is your best friend."

"I cannot continually ask Reggie's help whenever I find myself in difficulty."

"When have you ever?" Lizzie countered quickly.

"Never," grinned Sir Antony, "and I do not intend to begin now."

"So you content yourself with frustrating me."

A small furrow skittered across his forehead but he decided to smile. "I content myself with boring you telling woeful tales simply to have an excuse to gaze at you," he declared.

"You do not need an excuse, nor pretty words," she replied, but felt another blush arise and avoided his gaze nonetheless.

"Thank you. I am not proficient in discovering either."

This time the ensuing silence was so vastly comfortable that Lizzie awoke with a start and a frown at Childers's interruption.

"Your party has arrived, my lady," he announced discreetly from the doorway.

"Party? Oh! Yes! I had forgotten. Please tell Miss Bach that I shall be there at once. I'm promised for an outing in the park, I'm afraid," she apologized as an idea occurred to her. "Why not join us?" she asked brightly.

"I should like nothing more but I have another engagement," he explained, adding at her hurt expression, "with Mr. Gentry, my father's man."

"Oh, well then, I shan't keep you."

Lizzie could think of nothing more to add as Sir Antony possessed himself of her hands once again.

"I very selfishly have absolutely no desire to leave your company," he murmured, reading her thoughts, "and every desire to keep you from your friends."

"I am very selfish, too, sir," she returned, although she found normal breathing extremely difficult, "and I refuse to exist in the dark in regard to your affairs. I do not believe myself entirely impudent in thinking they concern me."

"Not entirely," he agreed.

"Please, Tony," Lizzie whispered, "won't you speak to Reggie?"

With a noncommittal smile, Sir Antony kissed her quite gently upon the lips and, finding the response warm and yielding, did so not once but twice.

"There is so much to tell you," Lizzie gasped as her head cleared, "and—"

"And you have people waiting," he reminded her.

"And I am a horrid creature for wishing them gone," she replied, laughing. "Tell me that you will attend Assembly tonight at Brooks's and I shall leave almost happily."

Sir Antony gave another noncommittal smile as the door closed behind her. The grin changed instantly to a grimace as he remained standing in the middle of the library.

He revolved once about the room as if committing its contents to memory. His eyes lingered upon the desk but the thought to write a note to the earl was banished as quickly as it came.

"Is there anything you wish, Sir Antony?" Childers asked quietly from his patient stance in the doorway.

"No thank you, Childers. I'm leaving." Sir Antony made for the exit only to stop alongside the servant. "You could tell me when you expect Lord Croyton to return?" he asked.

"It was my understanding that he went to meet you, sir," replied Childers.

"We missed each other," Sir Antony replied with a shrug.

The butler nodded his understanding and ventured: "Then I should say His Lordship would return as soon as possible—by the end of the week, perhaps."

"He won't stay in Bristol?"

"His Lordship is most particular about accommodations," the retainer sniffed. "Would you care to leave a message?"

Sir Antony returned to his earlier decision. "Thank you, no," he said. "Perhaps I'll see him when he returns."

He walked out onto Hanover Square and strode off down the cobblestone pavement. In a matter of minutes, he stood before a large red-brick building kept clean by the constant attendance of a multitude of workers. The windows sparkled in the afternoon sun and the large oaken door beckoned. The building contained the offices of Brown, Haverstock and Gentry, solicitors.

Sir Antony climbed the steps as his thoughts returned to almost three years previous.

The offices had not changed. Dark, panelled halls still gleamed in high polish, and the open entry permitted the light of day and the gentle breezes easy access but could not dispel the gloomy atmosphere which permeated the building. Sir Antony attempted to shrug off the feeling, to no avail. The place would always hold bad memories.

Mr. Gentry had been as helpful as possible that day in June after Sir Geoffrey died but there was no denying facts. His father, who possessed no head for figures, left his son an income of little over one hundred pounds per annum and a property in Kent which took almost every penny of that to maintain.

Sir Antony had gathered what he could spare and departed for the Americas. During his final days, Sir Geoffrey had invested quite heavily in property on the island of Jamaica. A small, yet purportedly high-producing sugar plantation was Sir Antony's only hope of restoring his flagging resources.

"I expected you sooner," commented Mr. Gentry as Sir Antony seated himself.

"I had personal business to attend to," the younger man explained and he examined the limpid blue eyes staring out of Gentry's worn, emaciated face. There were probably a few more wrinkles, but it would have been impossible to pick them out. The thin mouth smiled over perfect white teeth, for although Mr. Gentry was well over sixty, he still possessed the most marvellous teeth.

"Tony, my lad," began the soft voice, fainter with the years, "your last letter worried me. You sold everything?"

"For passage back." He laughed bitterly. "You were correct about the state of things there. The place was a shambles."

Once again, he recounted the tale which was becoming nauseatingly painful to him, merely concluding with a calm and simple "There was little I could do."

"You are too hard upon yourself," the lawyer replied, "the 'sins of the fathers,' as they say. I warned Sir Geoffrey of the risk he was taking—that the expenditures might not realize a profit. When your father latched on to an idea—no matter its worthiness—there was no dissuading him.

"I was encouraged when you wrote of a crop ready to market."

"Two harvests," corrected Sir Antony, and he smiled and added ruefully, "destroyed by hurricane the first season and drought the next. I am not a planter, sir, but I am enough of a gambler to recognize when the odds are against me. Jamaica and all such foolishness is behind me but I do not regret the experience. I came today—" he squared his shoulders "—to discover the exact state of my affairs."

Mr. Gentry nodded his head sagely, unsurprised at the request. "I can have the books brought up if you would like," he offered.

"Is that necessary?"

The solicitor chuckled to himself. "No, I have kept an eye on things for you. What is it you wish to know?"

Nervous energy brought Sir Antony up from his chair. He drifted towards the window as the old man's kind, sad eyes followed every move of his tall frame.

"I would like to know—" he stared out at the limited view of the world afforded by the window "—how much I could expect if I sold Brentshire now."

CHAPTER FIVE

"SELL IT? But, my dear boy, whyever would you wish to sell it?"

"How much?"

Mr. Gentry recovered from his shock and gave the young baronet a figure.

It was Sir Antony's turn to be dismayed. "Is that all?" He asked.

"If you were to sell now," explained the other. "The market is not at its best at present, I'm afraid. And then there is the condition of the estate—I've done what I could but the money simply isn't there. The amounts you receive from tenants barely cover costs.

"The main house is in desperate need of major repairs. I am constantly shocked at the state your father allowed it to get into. And the mill is, I'm afraid, in even worse shape."

"The mill? I had forgotten about that." Something fluttered in the back of Sir Antony's mind, but he was abruptly recalled to the present by the sound of Mr. Gentry still speaking.

"Oh, yes, the mill. I remember it when Sir Geoffrey and I were young," he said. "I don't believe it was being used even then. My goodness, that would be thirty years ago. I'm certain the building must be in ruins by now."

"How much would it cost to get the mill running again?"

This second shocking question was almost too much for the older man, and he gasped desperately for air to fill his ancient lungs.

"My poor, poor boy," he finally managed in a strangled voice, "dissuade yourself of any ideas in that regard. I wouldn't care to hazard a guess at the amount but I'm certain it would cost a small fortune and you haven't the money, in any case."

"True," Sir Antony admitted, "but it cannot hurt to ask. I intend to visit the place as soon as possible," he continued abruptly. "I would appreciate your making what arrangements are required for the sale."

"May I make a suggestion," begged Mr. Gentry, and he proceeded only at the other's stalwart nod. "I am quite fond of you, m'boy, and I should hate to see you make a mistake which you might regret. I never approved of your leaving England, but you were determined, so..." He let the sentence drop as Sir Antony stiffened.

"This is a different matter entirely. To contemplate selling off a family estate is difficult for most men, but for you I should think it would be impossible. I should hope it would be. I remember the joy in that house when you were a boy and your mother was alive. Oh, it was falling down even then, but for some reason no one could notice it."

His eyes brimmed with tears and he smiled as he relived distant memories. "You know, I never had a family of my own. I was always too busy when I was young and then suddenly I was too old. But I had a home; that house was home to anyone who stayed there."

He turned his eyes upon his client and concluded, "These are the wanderings of an old man, for which I apologize. But do this old man one favour—wait until you visit the place before you make any decision."

Sir Antony swallowed the lump in his throat with difficulty. "I will, sir, I assure you," he said.

"I'll have the books brought up now," Mr. Gentry said as he moved to an adjoining door. "There was only one item I could not allow to lapse, despite your instructions to the contrary," he confessed. "I have maintained your subscriptions to Brooks's and White's. You never know when you might find them handy."

Although Sir Antony could not approve of the solicitor's initiative at the moment, he was to suffer a change of heart by the close of the afternoon and after a thorough perusal of his accounts.

WHITE'S WAS ALMOST DESERTED as he entered and this lack of patrons pleased him immensely.

Unfortunately for Sir Antony, his peace was shortlived. No sooner had he settled himself in a large chair by the fire and taken the first sip from his correspondingly large glass of whiskey, than he found himself the object of attention from a rather large individual.

A constant frequenter of the genteel rooms, Mr. Harvey Forbisher plopped his huge bulk into the chair across from Sir Antony and exclaimed, "Russelford! I say, old chap, when did you get back? I thought you were to be out of the country for years. Surprising to see you. Couldn't take those rebellious colonies, what?" He laughed goodnaturedly at his own jest.

"I went to Jamaica, sir," replied Sir Antony with a sigh.

"Got a bit of catchin' up to do, don't you?" asked Mr. Forbisher and not waiting for Sir Antony's answer—which would not have been forthcoming at any rate—

droned on in the same vein, recounting events of interest from the past three years. His company was never appreciated as much as he felt was his due and he was far fonder of the sound of his own voice than any meticulous adherence to fact. He strayed from historical accounts quickly and was delving into the more intriguing and satisfying arena of human endeavours when Sir Antony interrupted him rudely.

"What did you say?"

Mr. Forbisher was always pleased at a chance to repeat himself and replied, unperturbed, "I was merely wondering if you'd had a chance to see Lord Croyton since your return. You were good friends, I understand."

"His lordship is out of town," Sir Antony answered.

"Well, well, that would explain it," cooed Mr. Forbisher as he digested this piece of information.

"Explain what?" asked an immediately wary Sir Antony, and he cursed himself for forgetting the rules of town conversation.

Mr. Forbisher, however, merely looked overjoyed at the chance to show off his own knowledge rather than glean any from the baronet. "Well, I really shouldn't say," he began, then overcame his reluctance in a trice and, leaning forward, lowered his voice confidentially, "but seeing as how you're a friend of the family, so to speak, I suppose it would do no harm to tell you. The whole town appears to talk of little else. Lady Elizabeth has become extremely partial to that Costain fellow's company."

Sir Antony racked his brain for the name. "Sir Rodney?" he queried.

"No, no. The son, Martin Costain. Didn't you go to school with him?"

"He was a year behind me."

"Well, he's not behind anymore—" Forbisher chuckled heartily "—if you understand me. Oh, yes, he's turned into quite a handsome little devil. And, I do mean *devil*."

Sir Antony's face hardened, but he controlled the edge in his voice. "You say Lady Elizabeth is seen in his company?"

"Constantly. It has surprised us all. I, for one, thought he would be after the Bach chit. All that money, y'know. Or maybe you don't know, being out of the country and all. At any rate, it seems he's turned his attention to Drenview's sister. This past week they've been inseparable. And now you tell me Drenview's out of town, which accounts for it. He would never approve if he knew.

"Although one can never be quite certain," he continued, vacillating. "Rather an odd fish, the new earl. Now, his father—there was a man! One always knew where one stood with him, a true out-and-outer. There'd be no doubt about what he would have to say on the matter. No doubt at all. Send Costain packing, he would. Be the thing to do."

"Why is that?"

Forbisher glanced at his companion sympathetically. "My dear fellow, you have been away too long. If you must know, Costain is the complete rake. A regular smasher. Hasn't got a sou to his name except what his father sends him and that he manages to lose in the first outlandish bet he can name.

"I even hear that the fellow's been in two duels already. Over—" he cleared his throat and drew still nearer "—the fairer sex, one of whom was supposedly married. I've often wondered who that could have been, but it's neither here nor there. Mind you, the man's a crack shot with a pistol. And I understand his sword arm is one of the best. I suppose it would have to be, considering the life he leads. Never a dull moment, what?''

Mr. Forbisher settled back and continued to expound: ''He's just come back from the Continent—no doubt they were glad to be rid of the scoundrel—and he took up with the Bach chit almost immediately. Strapped for cash I hear, probably decided it wouldn't do any harm to marry an heiress, especially one so easily wooed. Money in the bank, so to speak, with nary a pinch to one's purse in the process. Bach's got five daughters, y'know. Simple enough to latch on to one who doesn't get the attention a young female deserves. Costain's basically a lazy fellow, I hear, although I shouldn't mind telling you that he won't settle for anything less than what he sets his cap for—from what I hear, that is.

''Come to think of it, that might explain the switch to Lady Elizabeth. If one must marry an heiress, why not a beautiful one? It would certainly make life more pleasant, don't you agree?''

Startled by the expression on Sir Antony's face, Mr. Forbisher lost his train of thought. ''I say, dear fellow, you don't look quite the thing. Are you feeling all right? Must allow yourself to get adjusted, you know. Travelling is always horrendously upsetting. Try to avoid it, myself.''

Sir Antony downed the remainder of his drink in rapid gulps. ''I'm fine, I assure you,'' he said. ''You will excuse me, sir, it's been a pleasure seeing you again.''

''Well, really,'' Forbisher muttered, ''definitely shouldn't travel. Very upsetting.''

He ignored Sir Antony's abrupt departure and, scanning the room placidly, was rewarded by spotting two likely candidates for conversation.

STRIVING TO SALVAGE her own conversation, Valerie
Bach glanced up at the man riding beside her and smiled
shyly. "I think you're coming along marvellously, Mr.
Wallace."

The young man beamed. "Do you think so? Truly?"

Upon being assured that she did indeed think so, Mr.
Wallace straightened in the saddle. "To be quite honest," he said, "I thought I should never get the hang of
it. But now that I have, it's quite fun, you know."

Mr. Wallace had become a fair horseman in the few
days since that first embarrassing experience. He sat and
moved with more confidence and ease, and upon close
inspection it appeared that he had shed an inch from the
middle. Mr. Wallace was taking great pains to make
himself more presentable and had resigned himself to a
strict diet and exercise regimen. Since his exercise in-
cluded two hours a day on horseback, this adequately
explained his increasing expertise.

He mentioned none of this to Lady Elizabeth. If it did
not aid his cause, there was no need to feel more foolish
by confiding it to another. As each day passed, however,
his waistcoat loosened and his confidence grew.

Valerie noticed the change in her companion. He impressed her as sweet, with the kindest eyes she had ever
seen in a man. He knew what she was going to say before she said it, but he laughed at her jokes anyway and
always seemed to be smiling. It was a shame he was so
very quiet and shy, she thought, and that he would turn
red whenever she spoke to him. He didn't react that way
when Lizzie spoke.

She looked across the gentleman to the object of her
thoughts. Lizzie rode silently. She never spoke much
when Mr. Wallace was present, and thus forced Valerie
to attend to the social amenities. This afternoon was no

different but Valerie had known her too long not to detect the troubled preoccupation which she strove to conceal. Fortunately, Mr. Wallace was a comfortable man and did not object to the frequent lulls in conversation. She glanced up at him again from under her lashes and concluded that he was, indeed, quite sweet.

Lizzie never discussed the men in her life seriously. She joked and flirted outrageously; she laughed with them and at them but always with a sense of great fun. The recipient of dozens of proposals, she did not speak of them, for no man attracted her attention save one.

Valerie sighed as Mr. Wallace coughed significantly. Both ladies were unusually still and the silence made him uneasy. He tried hard to think of something to say.

"Will you be attending the Assembly tonight, Miss Bach?" he asked.

"Oh, yes. Mama is particularly set on going. I understand the Prince is planning to attend and Mama wishes to see him," Valerie replied gaily. "Lizzie's met him, haven't you, Lizzie?"

Hearing her name mentioned, Lizzie broke from her reverie. "I'm sorry, Val, did you say something to me?"

"The Prince. You've seen him?"

"Prinny? Yes, of course I have." Her face and voice registered annoyance at the question and she glanced away quickly.

"Oh, isn't that Aunt Martie over there?" She waved. "I really must speak to her. Continue riding, you two; I don't wish to spoil your fun."

Lizzie set her horse at an easy canter towards Lady Graneville's curricle and reprimanded herself sharply for her abrupt behaviour. She must apologize to her friends later, but all she could feel was a deep hollowness that made Sir Antony's return seem so unreal. She knew there were matters requiring his attention, but the few minutes granted her that afternoon merely stirred her craving for his presence rather than quenching it.

The couple watched her go with perplexed expressions.

"I've never seen her this way before," Valerie ventured.

"Perhaps she is unwell?"

"I don't believe she's ever been unwell," she admitted. "She's always so wonderfully brave and doing such daring stunts. There was the time she challenged Mr. Strawn to a duel because she said he had insulted her by calling her 'flighty.'"

"My God! Surely they didn't fight!"

Valerie could not stop giggling at the memory. "Yes, they did! Here, in the park. It was the dead of winter, so the weapons were snowballs at twenty paces. I'm afraid Mr. Strawn was laughing so hard that he lost quite badly. It didn't matter, though, because soon everyone who came to watch was in the middle of it. It was quite the best fun.

"When it was done, Lizzie told me the only reason she had challenged Mr. Strawn was that it was too beautiful a day to waste indoors, and she felt like playing in the snow. She's always doing such things.

"I don't know for certain, but I do believe Mr. Strawn proposed to her the very next day." Valerie sighed and added confidently, "Of course she would never accept anyone but—" Her eyes dropped instantly and she blushed a bright crimson at the realization of how close she had come to betraying her friend's confidence. "But . . . but I could be wrong," she ended lamely.

Unaware of the conversation revolving about her, Lizzie pulled alongside Lord Graneville and smiled brightly.

"Hello, Uncle Henry."

The tall, thin gentleman riding to the side of his wife's vehicle nodded briskly to his adopted niece. He rarely had anything to say and preferred to leave the talking to his more garrulous mate.

Lady Graneville glanced up at Lizzie's approach and scanned the girl's appearance rapidly.

"Lizzie, my darling! You look frightful!"

"And it's good to see you, Aunt Martie!" Lizzie laughed.

"Henry, help the girl down from that horse and into this gig instantly!"

The terse command was obeyed without protest, and Lizzie squeezed into the seat and met her ladyship's piercing eyes directly. She failed miserably to hold the gaze.

"I thought there was something wrong the other night and now I'm certain of it," the older lady said knowingly. "What have you been up to this time?"

"I haven't been up to anything. I'm just a little tired today."

"You—tired?! Harrumph!" snorted Lady Graneville. "Has that brother of yours returned yet?"

"No."

"Harrumph! What is this business with Costain? First, you're asking questions and the next you're never seen out of the man's company. Tongues are wagging, my dear!"

Lizzie smarted under her aunt's comments. "Let them wag!" she snapped. "I don't care!"

"You'll care soon enough. One day your careless behaviour will get you into serious trouble and then no decent man will have anything to do with you, beauty or not. And don't think your beauty will last forever. It won't. Then you never will be married."

"I don't wish to be married! I enjoy my freedom."

Her ladyship raised one eyebrow and pronounced, "Nonsense! You're almost twenty-one, not a girl any longer, mooning after some young cockerel with an endearing smile. Oh, I know all about Sir Antony Russelford," she added quickly at Lizzie's sharp intake of breath. "I haven't known you this long without learning a thing or two. Come to your senses, girl! The lad is completely unsuitable. Why, he's as shy, not to mention poor, as a churchmouse. What you need is a firm hand...a firm hand to take you in charge. Keep you out of mischief! I'll speak to Reggie about it the moment he returns. It's time the lad took some action about seeing you suitably placed."

"Aunt Martie, no!"

"He's shirked his duty long enough. It's becoming quite shameful. Imagine! Allowing you to make your own decision about something as important as marriage! Things were different in my day, I can tell you. Such wanton behaviour would never have been countenanced!"

Lizzie's cheeks burned as she recalled that afternoon's interview. What Aunt Martie would say if she knew how wanton her niece had actually been!

Lady Graneville eyed the beautiful girl beside her and her heart softened. She placed a comforting arm round Lizzie's shoulders and gave her a gentle hug.

"I'm thinking only of your own good, Lizzie," she said. "You'll come to see that in time."

Lizzie blinked back her tears and nodded. "Yes, Aunt Martie, I know you are," she muttered. "I simply don't know what to do. I feel as if it has been ages since I've been happy."

"Don't you worry, m'dear, everything will work out for you. It always seems to when you're young. Now you go back and join your friends. Have some fun and forget about that young man."

"Yes, Aunt Martie," she promised and felt ever more miserable for the lie.

"There, that's much better. Henry."

Lord Graneville strode forward and assisted Lizzie back upon her mount.

As she turned with a cheery parting wave, Lady Graneville bethought herself of one last order.

"Stay away from Martin Costain," she called.

Her ladyship watched the young rider gallop back across the park and she sighed heavily.

"Henry," she asked, "am I doing the right thing?"

Lord Graneville smiled fondly at his forceful wife. "My dear Martie, I think you were rather harsh on the girl," he replied honestly, adding with quick tenderness, "but I've never known you to do the wrong thing. I am curious, though. What was that business about not making your own decision?"

"I was speaking in general," countered her ladyship swiftly.

His smile grew broader and his eyes twinkled merrily.

Lady Graneville's lips twitched in response as her own eyes dropped beneath her husband's steady gaze. "You know very well I made my own decision," she murmured.

"For which I shall be eternally grateful." He bowed gallantly.

"Almost thirty years of marriage, sir, and you can still make me blush like a schoolgirl."

CHAPTER SIX

THE EVENING held a slight chill as Sir Antony stepped up to the entrance of Brooks's. The place was alive with people bustling to and fro, and the baronet wondered briefly if he had dressed appropriately. He felt distinctly out of fashion as he watched the dandies in their ear-high collars and skin-tight coats. He prayed to remain unrecognized and was not disappointed in his wish as everyone was far too involved in his or her own poise and appearance to spare but a quick glance at him.

He chided himself for being so foolish as to place any value in malicious rumours, but stood out of the main stream of traffic nonetheless and searched the assembled. He spied Lizzie across the ballroom floor. She held court—there was no other phrase to describe it—far from the main entrance.

Her golden hair was gathered delicately to one side and allowed to cascade in a waterfall of curls. The bodice and puffed sleeves of her pale pink gown were cut low, revealing a pair of milky white shoulders. He watched as she carelessly tapped her fan against an empty palm to the rhythm of the music.

Sir Antony noted wryly that she was laughing with the gentlemen flocked about her.

Lizzie smiled at Lord Bettlely with an élan she was far from feeling. She wished only to see Tony, and listening to these men prattle on so had given her the Headache.

She resolved for Valerie's and Mr. Wallace's sakes, however, that she would be as cheerful and gay as always.

She struggled to sound interested in Lord Bettlely's tale but, in truth, she possessed no clear recollection of what he had just said.

Seizing the opportunity granted by the young lord's self-satisfied preening, Mr. Costain bowed gracefully above Lizzie's hand. In a lilting voice, he asked, "Would you give me the honour of this dance, Lady Elizabeth?"

Lizzie blinked in surprise. She had no desire to jeopardize her tenuous relationship with Martin Costain and even less desire to dance with him. She assumed a conciliatory smile and choked upon her reply.

"Pardon me." Sir Antony edged his way forward and held out his hand. "You will excuse us, sir, but this dance is already taken. My lady?"

Lizzie's heart raced as she felt his strong fingers enclose hers. She was not so lacking in manners, however, to forget Mr. Costain, whom she favoured with an apologetic smile.

She glanced up at Sir Antony from under her lashes as he escorted her onto the floor. He looked unaccountably stern and his jaw was set in an unyielding profile.

The dance was far progressed before a word was exchanged.

"I forgot to ask earlier, how is Reggie?" Sir Antony began in what he hoped was a conversational tone.

"Fine," she breathed and felt her head spin. After all that had passed between them, he asked about her brother.

"I see you're as popular as ever."

Uncertain how to respond, Lizzie laughed the comment aside breezily. "I do seem never to be without a dance partner."

"Or two or three," he said sarcastically, and his jaw tightened. "I wonder then that you should have been so distressed this afternoon. I'll wager you have half a dozen proposals within a fortnight." The sharp words were spoken only to be instantly regretted.

"I don't want half a dozen proposals, thank you," she snapped, wondering at his inexplicable change of mood.

Luckily, the dance separated them at this moment, and when they were reunited, Sir Antony took a different tack.

Studying her downcast eyes and angry frown, he had never felt more miserable. "Lizzie," he said sternly, "I admit I was wrong—"

"You've changed your mind." The depth of joy expressed in those few words startled him. "You'll speak to Reggie."

"No," he replied quickly and firmly as all the new sparkle died in her blue eyes. "I was wrong," he explained, "to think that you would understand. I should have written sooner."

Lizzie moved away in a daze. Her lips froze into a polite smile for her fellow dancers, and when she found her hand once more in his, she had regained some measure of composure.

"I try to understand—" she held her voice in firm control "—but I cannot. It is as if I do not know you anymore."

"Lizzie," Sir Antony pleaded, "I'm only trying to be practical."

"And I'm not?"

"You don't receive the income from your trust until you're twenty-five. What should we do in the meantime? Let us be logical."

Lizzie brushed this objection aside. "Is that what concerns you so? Reggie's my guardian, if you can call him that, and he's never denied me what I've wanted."

Once more the dance intervened and it was Sir Antony's turn to be bitter when they came together again. "People would still think me a fortune hunter, and they wouldn't be far wrong."

"Stop being silly! Who cares what they think?"

She laughed at the realization that she truly did not care. All care for the proprieties vanished and she stared up into his face and spoke so quickly that she surprised herself by her boldness. "I've never made a secret of my feelings," she said. "I'm quite shamelessly throwing myself at your head. In case you haven't noticed, Sir Antony, I'm the one who's proposing."

The couple stopped dancing, and oblivious to everyone else in the room, the young baronet raised the lady's hand to his lips.

"I'm honoured," he whispered and shook his head with a sad smile, "but I cannot accept, Lizzie—not now."

"Not three years ago, not now, not ever—," she flung up at him. Then the look in his eyes stopped her. "Tony, no."

"I'm not doing this lightly." He spoke just as quickly. "I've thought a great deal—"

"No," she croaked, jerking her hand from his. "Is that what this is all about? Did you imagine that getting me angry would make a difference? It doesn't. I won't argue with you and I won't have you return just to say goodbye to me. I won't listen to it!"

"Lizzie—"

Blindly making her way off the dance floor, Lizzie found temporary sanctuary upon an empty terrace. There she gave full vent to her feelings, recovering only after several minutes to take stock of her situation. If she stayed on the terrace, she was certain to be discovered; yet there was nowhere else she was desirous of going. She remonstrated with herself briskly. This was neither the place nor the time to be missish.

She remained where she was and had no idea of the hour as she breathed in the cool night air and watched the dancers twirl. The swirling rainbow of colours in the ballroom possessed a hypnotic effect and she sighed deeply.

"Do you really think it will work?" a soft voice whispered in her ear.

Spinning about with a start, Lizzie stared into the smug face of Martin Costain.

"I wouldn't lay you odds myself," he said with a smile.

"I don't know what you're talking about, sir."

"Don't you? I rather thought it was your idea, but I may be wrong. I see I must be. I apologize. Could it be that your sudden interest in me stems from other motives?" he asked as he drew closer.

Lizzie stepped back instinctively.

"No, I didn't think so." Costain chuckled, and ignoring her, he turned to the window and contemplated the dancers serenely.

"You should know, of course," he began, "that Miss Bach and I have a mutual understanding. It grieves me that such a close friend as yourself should wish to disrupt our happiness. I don't expect you'll believe me. I'm afraid you've been listening to your brother's stories. But no matter, I should much prefer to be friends, wouldn't you?"

At Lizzie's prolonged silence, he shrugged and smirked at her. "Not even for Valerie's sake?" he asked.

Why did this man remind her of a snake? Lizzie thrust the image from her mind and cursed herself for being so obvious. She had flirted too outrageously with him of late and pushed Mr. Wallace too much into the foreground. It had all been too late in the game.

She found her voice at last. "Valerie is a very dear friend, Mr. Costain. The last thing in the world I want is to see her hurt."

"Upon that much we agree."

"Do we?" She had little to lose by being blunt and she cautioned, "She believes she is in love with you, sir, and I'm afraid she's going to be very hurt when she discovers you don't return her affection."

Costain raised a shocked eyebrow. "You misjudge me, Lady Elizabeth. What makes you think I don't love her?"

"I know your type. You love only yourself."

He scanned her features quickly. "No doubt you've explained all this to Miss Bach."

"You know very well that I cannot, and hope to keep her as a friend."

"So instead you play games. Which brings me back to my original question. Do you honestly imagine that Mr. Dexter Wallace—" he uttered the name with a sneer "—can steal her affections from me? Or that you can entice me, especially when I've been aware of your game from the beginning?"

He bowed and leered at her openly. "I admit I've enjoyed playing immensely, but I do think we've reached the final throw of the die. How have you placed your bets, Lady Elizabeth?"

Lizzie swallowed hard as his cold, villainous brown eyes twinkled at her without a glimmer of mirth.

"You stand very close to losing a friend," his voice whispered slyly, "unless you reconsider."

Slowly, Lizzie's muscles loosened and her shoulders sagged downward in defeat.

"Shall we join the others, my lady?" Costain asked politely, relishing his victory discreetly.

The hand she placed upon his was numb. Everything had gone so wrong that day.

She dragged a smile across her lips as the couple entered the Assembly room and she allowed herself to be led to Mr. Wallace.

Costain released her hand and made a gracious leg. "Thank you for the charming conversation, Lady Elizabeth. You will excuse me," he added and spun about, striding away with a bouncy step.

Dexter Wallace gave one glance at Lizzie's face as she stared after Costain. "I told you it wouldn't work," he said dismally.

"Oh, I'm so sorry," she breathed.

"All she talks of is him, but I do think she likes me."

"You could still talk to her. Tell her how you feel," urged Lizzie.

"To what purpose? She spoke so much of coming tonight and she hasn't made an appearance yet. I've made fool enough of myself, I think."

Mr. Wallace grasped her hand. "I do appreciate everything you've done, Lady Elizabeth," he said. "I realize it has not been easy but I will treasure every moment. I've had a chance to know her better and to love her all the more for it. Unfortunately, I've neglected my uncle's business by staying in London. I shall leave at the end of the week."

With a sad parting smile, Dexter Wallace left the Assembly rooms at Brooks's.

IF THINGS WERE GOING poorly for Lizzie, she was not alone in Fate's black books.

The Earl of Drenview arrived in Bristol a day late. This alone would have frustrated most men, but his lordship's only comment upon hearing the news was a bland "Oh."

After further contemplation, however, he declared almost joyously, "I knew there was something wrong with Lizzie's timin'!"

His joy was short-lived and his equanimity strained when he learned that, for some reason known only to the denizens of the seafaring trade, the harbour was teeming with life. It was as if every ship in the mercantile fleet had decided to make Bristol its port. Accommodations were not to be had.

"Well," his lordship pronounced, after mulling over the latest news for a full ten minutes, "there's really nothing to keep us here."

His silence had almost sent his valet into nervous hysteria at the thought of being stranded on the streets of Bristol, and Roberts heaved an emotional sigh of relief at the Earl's next words.

"Take us home, Spaulding," said Lord Croyton. "And please enquire at any inn you pass for lodgings." He paused and qualified: "Except, of course, if it's the one we stayed in last night. That linen could not have been aired."

"Certainly, My Lord."

Spaulding despaired of ever finding lodgings after the fifth inn rejected his cargo and the sun was well set behind them when he decided to forgo a place to sleep and head straight for London. He allowed the horses to slow and the methodical clip-clop of their hooves on the rough road combined with the churning of the wheels produced a lulling effect within the coach.

His lordship nodded as the constant stopping and starting at every inn ceased and the stillness of dusk fell.

Roberts remained awake. It was he, therefore, who caught the first glimpse of the figure in the bushes.

It rose up as a loud bang resounded and the figure instantly dove back under cover.

Spaulding jerked the reins and brought the carriage to an abrupt halt, which sent Lord Croyton spilling haplessly into his valet's lap.

"Wha-?" The rudely awakened earl straightened.

"Highwaymen, sir," whispered Roberts as he searched desperately for a weapon. The holsters on each door, built for the late earl's fine riding pistols, were empty.

Lord Croyton peered out the window. "Bother," he drawled.

"Hands up!" a strident voice yelled from the underbrush. "Drop those reins! You—in the coach—step out!"

The duo in the carriage followed orders, although Roberts, hanging back against the security of the coach, sneaked a glance up at Spaulding. The coachman had dropped the reins and held his hands as high as they could go.

The figure in the bushes rose again and came forward slightly to level a pistol at the earl's chest. "Hold yer fire, men," a voice said to the bushes as the figure continued its cautious advance.

In the early evening light, the shape took the form of a short, stockily built man wearing a large cap over his head and a dark mask covering his lower face. All that was visible was a pair of very dark, forlorn, houndlike eyes peeking out from under bushy eyebrows. The man approached to within three feet of Lord Croyton and stopped.

"All right, let's 'ave it," he commanded in a gruff voice and held out his free hand.

Lord Croyton raised his quizzing glass and carefully inspected the other as if he were no more than an errant fly upon his evening meal.

"Gad!" he exclaimed as the eyepiece dropped to dangle uselessly between two fingers. "It appears you were correct, Roberts," he pronounced. "This gentleman— and I use the term loosely—intends to rob us."

This pronouncement and the scrutiny upon which it was based produced immediate repercussions. The expectant villain retreated a step and blinked.

Then he broke from his speechless state with a grunt. "Aye, milord, so if ye'll just be 'andin' over yer blunt, I'll be gettin' out of yer way."

His lordship, however, was not one to be rushed. "I'm disappointed," he complained. "You're not at all what I would have expected."

"I ain't?" The highwayman's tone indicated that his present victim was certainly not what *he* had expected.

"Heavens, no!" asserted the earl. "You haven't the least look of the highwayman about you. Not vicious enough."

The footpad took umbrage. "I'm plenty vicious. Just cause I don' look it, don' mean I ain't."

Lord Croyton appeared heartened by this information. "Then I'm certain you must be, to be successful in this line of work. You are successful, I trust?"

His tone was conciliatory to the point of genuine concern, and Roberts breathed freer as the other's gun hand dropped.

"Well, as to that, milord, I don' rightly know," the bandit answered thoughtfully. "This bein' a bit out o' me line an' all. To be 'onest, this is me first time. An' I wouldna done it if I 'adna been desperate, like. Ain't had nothin' to eat for two days."

"Pity," his lordship commiserated, adding quickly, "that I should be your first victim. And the others?"

"Others?"

The earl waved his glass at the bushes.

"Oh!" The highwayman gasped his comprehension and the pistol rose instantly as his voice grew more strident. "They've all done this a 'unnerd times," he said. "So I don' think they'll be appreciatin' 'avin' to wait, sir. If ye be gettin' me meanin'."

He waved his fingers urgently.

Roberts cowered behind his lordship and fumbled for his purse. Nervously, he dropped it into the highwayman's outstretched palm and waited for Lord Croyton to follow suit. The peer, however, merely eyed the villain curiously and tapped his bottom lip with his quizzing glass.

"Milord," urged the highwayman with a sharp movement of his gun. "I'd as lief ye 'anded it over but I'm no scotch. I'll take it if I 'ave to."

"My Lord." Roberts added his hoarse whisper to the request.

Lord Croyton came alive as a frown of disgust crossed his features. "I object most strenuously," he announced. "Your manners, sir, could stand vast improvement. Certainly there is no cause to be insultin'!

"I suppose one must overlook such behaviour since this is your first time. And you may be within your rights to say I'm no judge, havin' never before been in this situation. However, manners are never out of place. If robbery is to be your trade, m'dear fellow, do try to be more polite about it!''

Roberts choked.

The object of this harangue blinked twice and the skin around his eyes crinkled.

Instead of discharging his weapon, however, the man bowed grandly to the earl. ''Pardon me manners,'' he begged contritely. ''Yer purse, if ye please, sir.''

''Better,'' approved his lordship as he handed over the bag in question.

The purse was heavy and jangled pleasantly in the thief's hand. He tossed it once and his eyes beamed.

''Thank ye, milord,'' he said and backed up to the shrubbery.

''One thing before you go, dear fellow,'' Lord Croyton called after him.

''A word of advice for the future,'' he continued off-handedly and, with a gracious bow, pointed his glass at the man's weapon. ''The next time you point a pistol at a man, you might make certain that it's primed.''

The footpad glanced down quickly and his expressive eyes bulged wide. Within seconds he recovered his senses and dived into the nearby stand of shrubs. A crash of underbrush resounded in the roadway and faded away in the distance.

''Shall we resume our trip, gentlemen?'' Lord Croyton asked, and motioned Roberts towards the coach.

Once the carriage was on its way, the valet spoke. ''My Lord, if you noticed the pistol wasn't primed, why did you give him your purse?''

Lord Croyton turned a bored face to his servant and considered the question a moment before replying, ''His men.''

''I don't believe he had any men,'' scoffed Roberts.

"No?" The peer sounded genuinely shocked at this suggestion. "But that would make the fellow out to be a liar. Really, Roberts, do you always think so ill of people?"

"But he's a thief!" the servant cried petulantly.

"Agreed—" Lord Croyton suppressed a yawn "—but I fail to see how that makes him a liar. Damnably inconsiderate of him, though, to interrupt my nap." He yawned again and settled back into the cushions. "Wake me when we reach the next town, Roberts. I suppose I must report this. Monstrous inconvenient, this whole affair."

With that proclamation, his lordship ended the discussion. Lord Croyton stretched out, his chin already fallen to his chest, as a steady rhythmic breathing filled the carriage.

CHAPTER SEVEN

THE NEXT DAY dawned like any other for the town of London. It was not to be a day like any other for everyone.

It was midmorning when Lizzie received the first note. Penned in an urgent hand, the message consisted of one sheet of paper and a smaller envelope addressed to Martin Costain. The note began:

Dearest Lizzie,
I am in the most desperate situation. Mama has absolutely forbidden me to see my darling Martin. She is being such a monster! She watches me constantly. I cannot even write this without her being in the room. When I told her it was for you she finally left. I enclose a note for Martin telling him all. Do be a dear, dear friend and see that he receives it. You are the only person I can trust. I shall be forever grateful!

Your loving Val

Lizzie turned the sealed envelope over in her hand as her mind spun in circles. There was nothing in the girl's note to cause suspicion, but a nagging doubt gripped her. Valerie was her friend and she should do what she asked of her. Or should she?

In the midst of her indecision, Childers announced a morning caller. "Sir Antony, My Lady."

Sir Antony entered the room as Lizzie rose from her escritoire, Valerie's note to Martin Costain still clutched in her hand, but momentarily forgotten.

"I'm sorry to disturb you," he said in a voice both stiff and controlled. "I won't keep you long."

He had not removed his caped greatcoat upon arrival and now pushed it back over his shoulders to reveal a plain dark spencer and buckskin riding breeches. The severity of his attire only accentuated the length of his frame and the brilliance of his blue eyes.

Lizzie spared no thought for the lovely picture which she presented. Her light blue morning dress swirled delicately as she rose to greet him, heightening the skylike colour of her own questioning eyes. The sun danced across her curls and framed her face in a golden glow. Her lips parted slightly in surprise at his visit, and a faint blush rose to her cheeks.

Seeing the clenching of Sir Antony's jaw as a sign of his stubbornness and disapproval, Lizzie smiled crookedly and spoke with false bravado. "Sir Antony, you surprise me. Have you come to say goodbye again?"

"I've come for two reasons," he answered shortly.

"Which are?"

"To tell you that I am leaving London for a week, possibly two. I'm returning to Brentshire for a look at the property."

"You *are* saying goodbye," she murmured and added lightly as she retreated to the window, "I wish you a pleasant trip then, sir."

"Lizzie, please," he pleaded, "try to understand."

"Indeed, sir," she replied, "as I explained, I do try. But I'm afraid I fail to see what possible interest I could have in your whereabouts."

Sir Antony's face lost all expression. "Deserved," he said, acknowledging her setdown. "I thought perhaps you might give Reggie a message from me when he returns. I should very much like to see him when I get back. If you have no objections."

Lizzie spun round to face him. "Who my brother sees would ordinarily have far less interest for me than your whereabouts."

"And in this instance?"

"That would depend." She hesitated, suddenly uncertain of revealing what must already be written upon her features. "That would depend upon your second reason for coming here today."

"My second reason," he explained slowly, "is to apologize. I admit I thought it would be easier if you hated me."

"I could never hate you."

"And I could never say goodbye to you. I am contemplating selling Brentshire," he confessed bluntly. At her shocked expression, he added with a stalwart nod, "That is how affairs stand with me, Lizzie. You wished not to be kept in the dark, remember?"

"Of course I remember. And I don't wish it, but—"

"I'm not saying goodbye to you—" he stopped her with a rueful smile "—although I cannot help but think you well rid of me. I visit Brentshire because it is my duty and I visit Reggie because you ask it, but above that, I guarantee nothing. Can you accept that?"

"Don't sell Brentshire, Tony," advised Lizzie quickly. "Stay in London. I don't know what could be keeping Reggie but I wish you would discuss it with him. Sometimes when it does look blackest, he says the most unexpectedly clever things."

"I will see him when I return," Sir Antony restated firmly. "Please tell him so."

"Certainly. Is there anything else you would like me to tell him?" She waved her hand expansively and Valerie's note fluttered to the floor between them.

Sir Antony bent to retrieve it and the name on the envelope caused him to pause. "No, nothing else," he said more harshly than he intended.

"Thank you." Lizzie reached forward only to find her hand seized.

"Thank *you*, Lizzie," he replied, raised her fingers to his lips, handed her the note and was gone.

Lizzie's whole body trembled. Why was he forever leaving her? Didn't he realize how difficult it was for her to see him, to keep her reserve and not let him see how much she was hurt?

She took several deep breaths, sniffed and stared at the note in her hand. If Tony had stayed a moment longer, she could have asked his advice on her problem, although it now seemed suddenly petty compared to his own. To deny Valerie unnecessarily for the sake of appearances...she knew how that felt, certainly. She would deliver the note and guarantee for her friend some happiness and peace of mind.

Lizzie sat down and wrote her own message to Costain. It was extremely short and explained how a friend had requested that she complete delivery of the enclosed. She placed both notes into a larger envelope, addressed it and rang for Childers.

That accomplished, she returned to the contemplation of her own miserable existence. She wondered vaguely when Reggie would return, for the house echoed without him.

She was still employed in this fruitless woolgathering an hour later when Childers entered with a second letter.

It was a response from Martin Costain and contained within the envelope another smaller one addressed to Miss Valerie Bach. Lizzie read her note with some trepidation but decided it was innocent.

My dear Lady Elizabeth,

I cannot express to you the joy I felt at receiving your note and its contents. True, understanding friends are extremely rare in this world and it is a privilege to have one. As you must know, I have been dealt a somewhat painful blow recently. I wonder, therefore, if you might do me the very great favour of passing the enclosed to our mutual friend. I hate to say goodbye in such a manner, but I fear there is no other way.

Your very humble servant,
Martin Costain

Faced with another dilemma, Lizzie had never felt more alone. But she would see Costain's note delivered and, without further thought, she marched to the servants' bell and within the hour had forgotten completely the note's existence.

IT WAS LATE that evening when a well-liveried coach drew up before the London residence of Lord Croyton and that travel-weary individual descended.

"Good evening, Childers." He smiled at the servant as he shrugged off his greatcoat. "It's certainly good to be home again."

"It is good to see you, sir," confirmed the butler.

"Yes." His lordship, distracted by the entryway mirror, straightened his tie. "Where is my sister this evening?"

"In the library, My Lord."

Opening the door with no little trepidation, the earl advanced only a small distance into the large room. "I'm afraid I have some bad news for you, Lizzie," he announced.

"I know," she responded from a chair by the hearth.

Lord Croyton blinked at her despondency, decided it was safe to close the door and walked farther into the room.

"Tony arrived in London almost three days ago," came the quiet explanation.

"Then you've seen him." His lordship stretched before the fire and soaked in the warmth on the back of his legs.

Lizzie nodded mutely and stared unseeing at the open pages of *The Lady's Magazine*.

"In that case, you've settled your disagreement and have no further need of my assistance," he predicted.

"Oh, Reggie!"

The cry was miserable enough to interrupt his lordship in midyawn.

"M'dear Lizzie, has somethin' happened?"

"Nothing you could help me with, I'm afraid." She rose quickly and began to pace to and fro. Her periodical dropped to the floor unheeded.

The words tumbled forth passionately. "He's being so stubborn, so...so odiously stubborn. I've been so foolish to think that he ever loved me. If he did, how could he have left in the first place? And now he's gone again. If it doesn't matter to me that he has no money or prospects, why should it matter to him? It's just so old-fashioned! He thinks he has to prove himself but he doesn't have to prove himself to me. I told him he was just being silly! I told him you would have absolutely no objections."

"I assume we're still discussin' Tony," her brother murmured as he bent to retrieve her fashion journal, "in which case, you're quite correct. You have been foolish."

Lizzie stopped pacing abruptly. "Reggie!" she cried. "Are you trying to say you *would* have objections?"

"I don't think it would matter to you if I did or didn't," he replied plainly.

"But how can you have any? Tony is your best friend! You've known him for years."

Lord Croyton nodded agreement. "True. A grand fellow all round."

"If you think that, how can you have any objections if he should wish to marry me?"

"But I didn't think he did," he objected. "Wish to marry you, that is. Or have I missed something again?"

Lizzie spoke as if to a child. "You said that I was being foolish," she pronounced.

"*You* said that. I merely agreed."

"Why am I foolish, Reggie?" Her voice cracked as the tears she had valiantly controlled for days threatened to burst forth. "To think that he loves me?"

Lord Croyton eyed his sister intently. "Odd's fish, Lizzie, do you *really* want my opinion?" he asked.

"Yes," she sniffed.

The idea appeared to be novel to the young earl. He regarded his sister with a raised eyebrow and twirled his fob chain between thumb and forefinger. He carefully placed her journal upon the mantelpiece, cleared his throat and began slowly in a soft voice. "When I agreed that you were bein' foolish," he said, "I was referrin' to everythin' you mentioned.

"First," he elaborated at her stony glare, "I think it's capital of Tony to want to make somethin' of himself, to prove his mettle, as it were, first rate. And if it means as much to him as it would appear and you love him, then shouldn't it mean as much to you?" He smiled dumbly. "I've always thought that was the essence of love—the noble sacrifice, what? Sheer nonsense, but hopelessly romantic.

"Second, no man likes to be called silly, especially by the woman he loves. And unless Tony has changed so drastically over the past three years, which I seriously doubt, then he does indeed love you." He waved his hand to signal his dismissal of the subject. "The reasons for which elude me."

Lizzie stared at her brother's completely blank expression in amazement. The need to confide in someone prompted her to further confession.

"I did something terrible the other night at Brooks's, Reggie. I wasn't thinking about proprieties or...or manners." She glanced furtively at him to gauge his reaction before continuing. "Tony asked me to dance and we got into a terrible row. Oh, Reggie, I asked him to marry me."

He watched her patiently and made no response.

Lizzie took a deep breath. "He refused. I became so vexed I just walked away."

His brow furrowed but it was a moment before he spoke. "Let me see if I understand you correctly," he said. "You proposed to him whilst you were dancin'. He refused—also while you were dancin'?"

"Yes." Lizzie hung her head in shame as a look of horror descended upon his features.

"Then you left him standin' in the middle of a crowded dance floor?"

"It wasn't that crowded," she defended quickly.

"Worse yet," he replied.

Lizzie wandered listlessly to the window. "If he does love me," she asked angrily, "why would he refuse, and why would he go away again so soon?"

"Dunno," said Lord Croyton with a shrug. "Appalled at your lack of manners, no doubt. Damme, Lizzie, leavin' your partner alone on a dance floor simply isn't done."

"It doesn't matter." She discarded her brother's opinion with a toss of her head and spoke all her doubts aloud. "He's changed so. Even you wouldn't recognize him. He's grown so cold and quiet and so...so tired. What can have happened? It hasn't been that long, has it? When he left I thought I would die and now that he's returned, I wish I had."

"Rather drastic, don't you think?"

"Oh, dear, I suppose so. Do you know how long I've waited to hear him say, 'Lizzie, I love you. Will you marry me?'" She looked up searchingly and met his blue eyes squarely.

"Yes," he answered, smiling, "I know."

The quiet conviction of his words startled her. "I didn't think you did," she confessed. "Aunt Martie knew, I don't know how. I thought because she was a woman and that somehow...well, somehow women seem better able to tell these things. Have I made such an obvious fool of myself all these years?"

"No, not obvious. But I am your brother, remember? I doubt there's much about me which escapes your attention. If I could help you, I would, but there's not much I can do at present."

"Thank you," she muttered.

Lord Croyton broke the ensuing stillness with a cough. "Did you say Tony's gone again? Where to?"

"Brentshire." Lizzie collapsed upon the window seat, completely spent. "He said he'd be gone a week, perhaps two, and he'd see you when he returned.

"Reggie!" she exclaimed suddenly, interrupting her brother in the process of taking a pinch of snuff. "Would *you* buy Brentshire?"

"Can't," he replied without a blink. "Ain't for sale."

"It might be. That's why Tony went there. He might sell it."

"Sell it? Devil take it, Tony without Brentshire is like a gentleman without—" he glanced with distaste at the snuff between his fingertips and returned it to the box "—like a gentleman without a decent pinch—utterly *devastated*."

"But he wouldn't be without it," explained Lizzie quickly and gleefully. "You would buy it and then give it back to him and he would have all the money he needs. It's marvellous! Why didn't I think of it sooner?"

"Why should I wish to give it back to him if I purchase it?"

"Because you're not purchasing Brentshire to keep it."

"I'm not? Well, of course I'm not. Ain't for sale." His lordship dismissed the idea and his mind drifted to other subjects. "Let me tell you about my trip to take your mind off this morbid track. Arrived in Bristol a day late, wouldn't you know." Lord Croyton's tardiness was notorious. "Not a place to be had for the night—quite frightful, it was. Naturally, we could only turn round and start back.

"Then, what must happen—" he warmed to his tale "—just when I was almost asleep—most inconvenient timing, it amazes me still—we were stopped by a gang of thieves. Roberts insists there was only one, but really, you never know about these things. One cannot be too careful. I remember...."

Absorbed with the possible permutations of her elegantly simple plan, Lizzie was abruptly brought to attention. "Reggie, there's a carriage pulling up," she remarked casually.

"Fine. At any rate, this fellow pops out of the bushes—"

"It's stopping here. They're unloading a trunk..."

Lord Croyton resigned himself with a sigh. "Really, Lizzie, and you talk about *my* spying."

"Oh, my goodness, it's Margaret!"

CHAPTER EIGHT

"Margaret?"

Oblivious to her brother's query, Lizzie dashed from the room. She recognized the Bach's abigail, who often accompanied Valerie on outings, and felt a sickening weight in her stomach that only boded ill. She chided herself for acting as a go-between with Valerie's notes and reached the front hall as Childers was about to open the door.

"Show Margaret into the small parlour, Childers," she instructed and disappeared back into the library to find the earl nonchalantly leafing through the pages of her magazine.

He looked up as she entered. "I will never understand how you women can abide these horrid fashions. Back to hear the rest of my story?"

"It's perfectly dreadful, I'm certain," she fretted.

"Oh, I shouldn't say that. Although there was a moment or two when I was convinced poor Roberts would faint. And I don't know how much longer Spaulding could have kept his arms up. But all in all, the fellow wasn't too horrid—for a rogue, that is. Although I've never met one before, so I am no judge. Sink me, it does always seem to come back to that."

"Something has happened."

"Well, of course somethin' has happened—monstrous dull story if nothin' happened," he remarked crossly.

"Oh, Reggie, do be quiet! Can't you see I'm thinking?"

Lord Croyton tossed the magazine onto a small table. "In that case, m'dear, I shall leave you to your thoughts. I really must do something about this dust." At this point, Childers appeared. "Ah, Childers, do see that a cold supper is put out for me."

"Yes, My Lord. I believe Roberts has prepared your bath, sir."

"Marvellous. Happy thoughts, Lizzie."

Childers waited until his lordship was out of earshot. "I have put the lady," he said with a faint sniff, "in the small parlour as you requested. May I ask, Lady Elizabeth, if you are planning a trip?"

"Why?"

"The lady—" he sniffed again "—mentioned leaving in the morning and that the trunk should be put with 'her mistress's other things.'"

"Thank you, Childers."

The abigail stood by the small fire warming her hands when Lizzie entered.

"Hello, Margaret," she greeted her warmly. "How are you?"

Margaret made a startled and cautious curtsy. "I'm fine, milady. It's most kind of you to ask. Miss Valerie has probably told you about the present, but I'm very much afraid I couldn't find it anywhere."

"Present?"

"Oh, she didn't tell you. I don't suppose I should have, but, there, it's out and what's to do about it? I suppose she'll be upset, the sweet darlin', but I did look every-where for it.''

"I'm positive you did, Margaret. And there's no harm done, truly."

"Thank you, milady. It's most kind. I don't want to be keepin' you, so if you could see Miss Valerie's told that I'm here I'll just go on up and see to her things."

Lizzie took a deep breath.

"Please, Margaret, why don't you sit down first. I'd like a chat with you."

For all the warmth and reassurance Lizzie put into her voice, Margaret baulked and her eyes grew wider. "Somethin's happened to me angel!" She cried. "I knew it the minute I walked in, I did, the way your man looked at me odd like. I'd die if anythin' happened to her. Is she all right, milady?"

"Please sit down, Margaret."

The servant needed no further encouragement, and collapsed upon the settee, never removing her eyes from Lizzie's face.

"There, that's better. You're very fond of Miss Val-erie, aren't you, Margaret?"

"Like she was one o' me own. She's the sweetest one o' the lot. But she's done something terrible, hasn't she?"

"I think so."

"She's not here, is she?"

"No. But if you tell me everything you know, we'll be able to help her."

Tears rolled down the maid's cheeks. "Oh, I don't know nothin', milady," she wailed. "She was so happy this afternoon when your letter came."

"My letter?"

"Yes, milady. The one invitin' her to Valstry for the month. It was just the thing for her, her feelin' so low and all. It came this afternoon and it perked her right up it did.''

Lizzie settled back into her chair as she commanded, "Tell me more about this letter."

"Why, I don't know much. Only that we was to come here 'cause we would be leavin' so early in the morn for your ladyship's estate. Then on the way over Miss Valerie couldn't find the present she was bringing your ladyship. She'd left it on her dressin' table. She was sore upset. So I went back to get it for her. And now she's gone.''

"Oh, Madam will never forgive me for this!''

"It's not your fault, Margaret.''

"Oh, no, you don't understand! Madam told me 'specially to keep a close eye upon Miss Valerie. And now this...! Whatever am I to do? And her in my charge less than an hour. Oh!''

Lizzie let the woman weep for a few minutes before speaking boldly. "Don't worry, Margaret. I shall think of something.''

"Do you think you can get the poor lamb back? Do you know where she went?''

"I have no idea," she admitted. "I want you to stay here, Margaret. Childers will bring you something to calm your nerves. Don't worry. I'll find Miss Valerie.''

"Oh, I hope so. I do hope so.''

Lizzie left the teary woman and climbed the stairs two at a time. She met Childers on the landing. "Childers, take some sherry into the small parlour for Margaret,'' she instructed him briskly. "See that no one disturbs her. Make the necessary preparations. I'll be leaving for Valstry tomorrow morning.''

"Will His Lordship be joining you?''

"No. Have Spaulding bring the coach round with fresh horses. Now, please."

"Now?"

"My brother and I will be going out immediately," explained Lizzie. "We will return later tonight."

"Very well. His Lordship's supper?"

"It will have to wait!" Lizzie called back as she ascended the remaining steps.

She entered her brother's bedchamber without knocking.

His lordship, having completed his bath, was dressed in a full-length gold brocade dressing gown. He seated himself before his dressing table, both eyebrows raised at his sister's flushed and unceremonious entry, and complained, "Damme, Lizzie, you could knock."

"Get dressed, Reggie! We're leaving!"

Lord Croyton sighed profoundly but followed his sister as she flew breathlessly into her boudoir. He closed the door quietly, leaned against the jamb and waited to attract her attention.

"The brown travelling dress, Mary!"

"Where are we going?" he asked patiently when her maid departed.

Her evening frock landed on the floor in a heap, revealing a single silk petticoat on a trim figure. Lady Elizabeth had never worn a corset in her life.

"Gretna Green," she answered.

Lord Croyton grinned appreciatively. "Won't do, m'dear—brother and sister, y'know."

Lizzie snorted in disgust. "I'm serious, Reggie. Valerie Bach has eloped with Martin Costain. We have to stop them!"

"Devil a bit, I do seem to miss things. What has their elopement to do with us?"

"I'm responsible for it," she declared emphatically.

"You? If you're responsible for it, then why do you wish to stop it? You're not makin' sense."

Mary returned at that moment with the brown dress and assisted Lizzie into it. "Please, Reggie," she pleaded through her twistings and turnings, "I'll explain everything on the way. Just do get changed."

"I don't suppose—" he hesitated "—that this could wait till after I've eaten?"

"No!"

"I rather thought not," muttered Lord Croyton, and he returned to his room to do as he was bade.

LESS THAN AN HOUR LATER, the earl and his beautiful sister were speeding through the streets of London toward the Great North Road and Gretna Green. The nocturnal trip had been taken hundreds, perhaps thousands, of times by the star-crossed, the misunderstood and the desperate—just slightly more often than it was travelled by the outraged relatives of the aforementioned.

Silence prevailed until the jostling which marked London travel ceased. They left the boundaries of the city and were on a straight, albeit far from smooth, road north.

Lord Croyton stretched his legs as best he could but was unable to find comfort. He cleared his throat.

"Now then, Lizzie, you're goin' to explain...?"

The girl clasped her hands in her lap and looked out into the night. In a subdued voice, she related every detail of her activities since her older brother had left London for Bristol.

"So you see why I feel responsible," she concluded with a sigh. "If I hadn't forced Mr. Wallace and myself between them, if I hadn't passed on those notes, none of this would have happened. Why can I never let well enough alone? Valerie told me in her letter that her father had forbidden her to see Costain. It was idiotic of me not to suspect his sudden contriteness. He had this in mind all along and I couldn't see it. I am such a miserable creature."

His lordship offered no comments, made no criticisms and asked no questions during the narrative. Now, he spoke very softly from his corner of the coach. "Where do you find the energy?" he asked. "I should be exhausted. Come to think of it, I *am* exhausted."

He reached forward and took her hand. "We will find your foolish friend," he whispered, "return to London, and I shall have my supper—with your permission, that is."

"Oh, Reggie—" Lizzie squeezed his hand and smiled through her tears "—you are the most marvellous brother."

A cambric linen was shoved into her palm as her brother's rich voice issued forth from the shadows.

"Shame on you," he said, "for doubtin' it."

The duo continued their journey in silence and the miles flew past the window. There was no word along the way of a couple matching the description of the pursued, and Lizzie, frantic with worry, began to despair of catching their quarry.

"Do you think, Lizzie?" Lord Croyton ventured solemnly, "that you could be wrong? That they're not headed for Gretna Green, after all? It is very possible they went in the opposite direction—to Dover."

Lizzie was spared from giving voice to her worst fears as a loud shot brought the coach to a jolting stop and sent her flying into her brother.

A voice from the darkness boomed out at them. "Hands up, if ye please! You—in the coach—be so kind as to step out. Hold yer fire, men!"

The couple in the chaise obeyed the harsh commands and as he helped his sister to descend, the earl stepped inadvertently into the amber circle of lantern light.

A hearty guffaw was heard instantly and a man on horseback, dressed entirely in black save for a small strip from his forehead to the bridge of his nose, rode forward.

"Blimey!" the outlaw exclaimed. "If it isn't hisself!"

Lizzie froze in midstep to the ground. "Reggie! Do you know this man?"

"Unfortunately," he murmured and added brightly; "You're lookin' prosperous. I trust things have improved for you?"

"Oh, aye. Couldna get much worse, now could they?" The highwayman's deep voice resounded with mirth. "In fact, I should be thankin' ye, milord, for this beautiful beast—" he indicated his steed "—an' for yer good advice."

Lord Croyton bowed magnanimously. "It was nothin', I assure you."

"Come, come, milord, too modest by 'alf." The voice laughed brimmingly.

"May I ask what you're doing on this route?" his lordship queried conversationally.

The rogue's manner lost all pleasantness. "Things got a mite warm on the Bristol road," he replied. "Some chap reported me!"

The earl *asked* solemnly. "Hardly sporting."

"No, sir," the other promptly agreed, pleased at the gentleman's obvious perception, "not sportin' at all, if I say so meself. 'Specially considerin' how agreeable I've been an' all. I took yer advice to 'eart, I did." His eyes danced as he waved his pistol, only to grow suddenly quiet and glance at the weapon speculatively. "Of course, I havena had much chance to use it other than what to stop carriages wi'. People seem almost 'appy to give up their blunt to a fella what says 'please' and 'thank ye.'"

His attention returned to the peer. "So if ye wouldna mind . . . ?"

"This is becoming monstrous expensive," objected Lord Croyton with a frown.

"Please, just give him the money, Reggie." Lizzie was fidgeting behind him. "We have to get going!"

A playful wink came from the outlaw as his voice dropped conspiratorially. "The lady's in an 'urry, mi-lord," he said.

"The lady is my sister." His lordship's every syllable dripped icicles.

"Beggin' yer pardon, Yer Lordship...milady. It's jus' that seein' as 'ow yer in an 'urry an'... it bein' night an' all and ye headin' north an'...I knows 'ow the lay aboot these thin's is an'...." The bandit's apology dwindled miserably and his eyes assumed the appearance of an errant dog beseeching its master for forgiveness.

Lizzie felt sorry for the pitiful creature. "It's quite understandable," she said sweetly, ignoring her brother's curious expression.

"Kind of ye, mum," the other said, brightening.

Lord Croyton removed his purse and contemplated it serenely. "I wonder," he asked, "if you might spare me a guinea or two—for expenses?"

"I'd be right proud to, sir," he said and, becoming suddenly magnanimous, added, "Take three."

"Kind of you." The earl transferred the coins to his waistcoat pocket.

"Not at all, sir. Least I could do. I'm 'appy to say, milord, that I'm right pleased it was you what stopped and not that last un. The bloke like as near blew me 'ead off, 'e did. Shame though, right fine setup, it were. Would've been a tidy pinch if they hadna got away. The finest matched greys, I've ever set me peeps on—an' I've seen more'n me share, mind ye."

Lizzie grabbed her brother's arm. "Costain has matched greys, doesn't he?" She asked and turned to the thief. "Did you rob them, too?"

The man shook his head patiently. "Wi' all due respect, milady, I canna rob 'em if they don' stop."

"That's them, I'm sure of it! And they're getting away!"

"Won't be goin' much farther," the highwayman volunteered, "if I ken anythin' aboot 'orses."

"What do you know about horses?" Lord Croyton asked, ignoring his sister's urgent tugs.

"I was in the King's Army fifteen years," the outlaw admitted proudly. "Spent the entire time in the 'orse brigade. Got a way wi' the beasts—don' unnerstand it meself, but there it is. Don' you worry, them greys might look prett'ly matched, but their timin' is all wrong. Weren't in step like they shoulda been. Pullin' against each other, they was. Makin' 'em right tired, 'specially bein' pushed like they was. Not like yers, sir—a right spankin' set ye've got there, milord."

"Thank you."

"When did they come by?" blurted out Lizzie.

"'Alf an hour, no more. He was comin' up the side road but I 'spect 'e'll be 'avin' to pull into the Bull & Crown fer fresh 'orses. Ye should be able to catch 'em easy."

"Let's go, Reggie!" Lizzie sprang into the coach without assistance.

About to follow, the earl was halted when the loquacious highwayman cleared his throat meaningfully. "Beggin' yer pardon, milord," he said and eyed the purse in the peer's hand, "but I think ye forgot somethin'."

"Oh, yes." Lord Croyton weighed the prize judiciously and smiled apologetically. "Forgetful of me, what?"

"Quite all right, sir."

His lordship strolled over to the bandit, but hesitated before dropping the bag into his waiting palm.

"I do hope," he remarked wistfully, "that this isn't going to become a habit."

"Oh, no, sir. The last time, I swear." His brow furrowed slightly and he leaned forward and confided in a solicitous undertone, "But if ye wouldna mind a bit of advice from the likes o' me—" he jingled the purse with vigour "—I wouldna be carryin' so much blunt if I was ye. Honest men are 'ard to find in these parts."

"So I've heard," his lordship replied dryly.

The highwayman's eyes twinkled with delight as he jerked his steed about and crashed into the underbrush. A brief reciprocating smile flitted across the earl's face before he rejoined his sister in the coach.

"Turn into the Bull & Crown, would you, Spaulding?" he called up to the driver.

"Really, Reggie," Lizzie complained as he climbed in, "where do you meet such people?"

Lord Croyton opened his mouth to respond, only to close it again, speechless, and settle back into the shadows with a small sigh.

CHAPTER NINE

VALERIE BACH PACED the length of the Bull & Crown's cozy private salon. Valerie was not interested in the warmth from the brightly burning fire in the hearth or the overstuffed chair beckoning to her weary limbs. Valerie was very worried.

Martin's beautiful greys had wearied early and he was arranging their replacement. The thought of pursuit was the furthest thing from her mind, however, for she was having second thoughts about the entire affair. Martin had been the perfect gentleman. He had not pressed her; yet somehow he had not acted as she expected a fleeing lover to act.

Whenever she caught a glimpse of his face in the flickering light through the carriage window it held a look of absolute triumph. A shiver ran down her spine as she recalled it, and she wondered if she had been wrong to allow herself to go this far.

If it was not too late to turn back, how to manage it? She spun about the room frantically, like a caged animal, but could devise no means of escape.

Desolate, she finally sank into the chair and turned mournful eyes upon Costain as he entered.

"It should only be a few more minutes and we'll be on our way again," he said and removed his greatcoat, tossing it and his gloves and hat upon the nearest table.

"You're looking frightfully pale. Let me have the landlord bring you something to drink."

"No," she returned quickly. "I don't want anything to drink, thank you."

"Don't be silly. You could use one and, frankly, so could I." He made a move to carry out his desire but was stopped by a tearful plea.

"Martin, I don't want a drink—truly. I...I just want...I mean..."

It had been a long day and Costain's nerves were frayed. The highwayman had shaken him more than he cared to admit and his greys, which he depended upon and had purchased at tremendous cost, were being replaced much too early in the trip. No doubt a very furious father was hot upon their heels as well.

Never a very patient man, he spoke sharply to the frightened girl. "Out with it," he commanded. "Have you something to say or not?"

Valerie's eyes were wide with fright.

Costain bit his tongue, reminded himself curtly that he did not have her yet and assumed what he knew to be his most reassuring smile. "Now, there," he cooed, "a little bit of horse trouble and I lose my manners entirely. I apologize. Now, what is it you wish to say? I promise I shall do whatever you ask and I won't bite your head off."

"I want—" Valerie fought to keep her voice level "—you to take me home."

The smile slowly disappeared from Costain's face, to be replaced by an ugly curl of his upper lip. His eyes hardened as they penetrated deep into her own. When he finally answered, his accent was rough.

"You're joking."

"Please," she choked out.

He strode up to her chair and laid a hand on each arm. Valerie sank back into the cushions as he leaned his body towards hers and whispered menacingly, "There is no going back, m'dear, and the sooner you realize that the better. We're going to Gretna Green and you are going to become my wife. Then we shall see just what your father has to say about it. If I were you, I'd be prayin' he welcomes us into the family, or the marriage, I fear, will not be a prosperous one."

Valerie's breathing came in shallow gasps; her face was flushed and her eyes burnt by the intensity of his gaze.

"I trust," he continued smugly as her lashes dropped, "that I make myself clear?"

Too upset to speak, Valerie jumped as the door to the salon banged open.

"Lizzie!"

Costain's victim extricated herself from the chair before he could react and flew across the room into her friend's arms.

"Oh, Lizzie!" she cried. "I'm so sorry...I'm so happy to see you! I've made such an awful mistake! Can you ever forgive me?"

Lizzie coddled Valerie in her arms as if she were a child and it was several moments before she had sufficiently quieted the girl to give attention to Martin Costain.

That gentleman surveyed the touching scene with his arms folded across his chest and a cynical leer upon his lips.

"Good evening, my lady. You'll forgive me if I'm surprised to find you chasing after errant friends alone."

"Oh, but she's not alone," drawled Lord Croyton as he stepped into the room and gave the other man a cursory glance through his quizzing glass.

"Lizzie—" he addressed his sister "—I've engaged a small room at the top of the stairs. I thought perhaps the two of you might wish to...freshen up?"

Lizzie led her unresisting charge away as Lord Croyton closed the door behind them.

"This is an even greater surprise." Costain's smile broadened. "I had heard you were in Bristol, my lord."

"I had only just returned when Lizzie insisted upon this short trip," explained his lordship, moving to stand before the fire.

Costain watched the peer warily through glittering eyes. "And like an obedient brother you came," he sneered condescendingly. "I congratulate your sister upon her persuasiveness. I know how loath you are to travel."

"Quite," the earl agreed, unheedful of Costain's smirk. He continued apologetically, "Lizzie was most determined. It seems Miss Bach is a very good friend."

"So you involve yourself in something which is none of your concern."

"Frankly, between the two of us," confessed Lord Croyton, "I should have preferred not to, but there, I'm afraid one's manners are the first to go in a situation of this sort." He made a florid gesture, and his snuff box appeared magically in his hand. He partook of a tiny pinch with precise, graceful movements and, once satisfied, snapped the lid closed abruptly and returned his attention to his companion.

"Besides, it is my understanding that you used my sister quite shamefully in the pursuit of your..." He waved his handkerchief expressively.

"And you're here for satisfaction, no doubt," Costain replied with a laugh.

Lord Croyton's quizzing glass shot up. "Odd's fish, sir!" he exclaimed. "You think I want to fight you? Your reputation precedes you and I fear I lack your... experience. Also—" he brushed his sleeve distractedly "—I positively abhor the sight of blood—especially mine!

"No," he continued after a pause, "I am here primarily as an observer, albeit a concerned one. It seems Miss Bach was on her way to spend some time with Lizzie, and somehow—" he shrugged to indicate his helplessness "—she became... waylaid? Most unfortunate. As a friend, Lizzie was worried, so naturally we came to make certain that the dear girl arrives safely at her destination.

"Knowin' that you're also a friend, I perfectly realize how concerned you must be as well," he concluded with a smirk. "But put your mind at ease, Lizzie and I will take special care of her."

"You think it's that simple?" Costain's anger rose precipitously in the face of this condescension. The man was becoming more than a mere annoyance. "Perhaps Miss Bach doesn't wish to go with you."

Lord Croyton gave this suggestion no little thought. "That is a possibility," he judged, "however, most unlikely. I recall she seemed rather distressed when we entered—hardly the attitude of one enjoyin' the company, what?"

A sly gleam lit Costain's dark eyes, and he spoke slowly to allow the message of his words to penetrate. "If I were to press the issue, the result would be different," he warned. "I'm surprised you'd wish to involve yourself in a scandal, friend or not. And if you think there won't be one, then you're very much mistaken."

Costain was rewarded by a momentary frown on the earl's face. His triumph was short-lived.

Lord Croyton smiled sympathetically and sounded bored. "Think carefully, my dear fellow," he advised. "What will you have gained by it? Consider the alternatives, if you will." He motioned deprecatingly with his quizzing glass. "If you leave now, no more need be said. You wouldn't have Miss Bach, but no one need ever know about this incident and you would be free to try again elsewhere. Although I can't say I find that prospect pleasin', one must learn to compromise.

"If you stay, then I should be forced to take action." He cleared his throat and admitted, "I find that prospect even less pleasin'. But there it is, and—heaven forbid—if you should be lucky enough to kill me—" he shuddered "—you would still not have Miss Bach but you would have the inconvenience of havin' to leave the country—rather in a hurry, I should think. The decision is yours." He moved to a chair and slipped into it. "I am, in either case—" he yawned "—entirely at your disposal."

Costain's eyes narrowed to thin slits as he cursed the other man's insolence. "I always wondered why I never liked you," he snarled.

A face devoid of all emotion examined him scrupulously. "Sink me," murmured his lordship, "I've never had a moment's doubt about the reverse."

There was a sharp edge to Costain's laughter as he flung his greatcoat over his shoulders. "Someday, Drenview, I think I would like to meet you, but, as you say, what will I have gained if I do so now?

"I bow," he said and did so, "to your superior argument, sir. Do give my regrets to the ladies."

At Costain's departure, Lord Croyton stretched his legs towards the fire and leaned his head back against the chair. The warmth of the blaze spread comfortingly over his limbs and he gazed into the flames for a few moments, closed his eyes and sighed contentedly.

Lizzie found him thus, sprawled peacefully before the hearth, when she cautiously descended the stairs an hour later. Inundated with a flood of self-recriminations, she had finally succeeded in convincing her distraught charge that all was not lost. They would return to London, leave the next day for Valstry and do exactly as the letter had proposed. No one would ever know what had truly happened, for Costain would certainly not reveal his disgraceful conduct and she trusted Reggie not to breathe a word. Why, he had probably already forgotten.

Not only that, Lizzie now mused wryly, he had fallen asleep.

"Reggie—" she gently nudged his shoulder "—Wake up."

The drooping eyelids lifted and she ventured, "Where is he?"

"Where is who?"

"Costain. Where is he?"

Lord Croyton yawned and stretched. "Dash it, Lizzie, why do you allow me to fall asleep in the chair so much? 'Tis monstrous uncomfortable."

Lizzie waited impatiently for her brother to make a quick survey of his surroundings. "Gad!" he exclaimed. "I thought it all a bad dream."

"Now, will you tell me what happened?"

"Nothin' happened. We talked and Costain left. He's probably halfway back to London by now, which is where *we* should be. I should like to get some sleep in my own bed, if you don't mind."

"What did you say to him? And what did he say to you?" she persisted.

"Can't we talk about this in the mornin'? I mean—"
he yawned again "—later in the mornin'? I don't wish to
complain, really, but as the night is gettin' on, I do think
we should as well."

"Very well," she moved, defeated, towards the door.
"I'll fetch Valerie. but you will tell me everything in the
morning, Reggie? Everything."

"Everythin'?" His lordship appeared stricken at the
thought. "Lud, Lizzie, you know this memory of mine!"

"Everything, Reggie."

The look she gave him brooked no argument and he
conceded with a dismal sigh, "Everythin'.

"Of what I remember," he added softly as she swished
triumphantly from the room.

The trip to London was made without mishap. There
were no highwaymen to slow their progress and the trio
reached Hanover Square in the very early hours of the
morning.

The house was far from quiet, however, as the staff
readied for her ladyship's departure later that day.

Margaret, true to Lady Elizabeth's request, had remained undisturbed in the small parlour, and she greeted
her mistress with tears of joy. The tears swiftly changed
to strictures as she assumed control of the situation and
ordered Miss Valerie to bed.

With Valerie safely shuttled away and Margaret in
good attendance, Lizzie plopped down dejectedly upon
the nearest settee.

"I shan't be able to move for a week," she confessed.

"I do hope you don't intend me to carry you up the
stairs?" Lord Croyton queried.

Preoccupied by the events of the night, Lizzie did not
answer but dropped her chin into a palm and stared at

nothing. "Fleeing to Gretna Green," she mused with a sigh. "Don't you think it's rather romantic?"

"Romantic!" his lordship exclaimed with genuine repugnance. "I should hardly call skippin' one's supper, riding at breakneck speed through the night, engagin' in desultory conversations with highwaymen and duellin' in public taverns *romantic*!"

Lizzie snapped from her dream with a laugh. "Oh, Reggie, you didn't duel!"

"No, thank God! But that is what you were meanin', isn't it?"

"You wouldn't do those things to protect the woman you loved?"

"I am, thankfully, not in love," he countered, "and if I were—heaven forbid—I should at least choose a woman with some sense."

"You don't *choose* a person to fall in love with." Her voice faltered slightly. "It just happens."

"It will not 'just happen' to me, dear sister. And now, I shall retire."

On his way to the door, his lordship walked over to his sister and cupped her chin in his hand. A slight smile played across his lips.

"I cannot say for certain," he whispered, "but I rather think *he* would. Good night."

Lizzie's eyes misted as she accepted the salute of a peck upon her forehead and watched him leave the room. There were times, she marvelled, when Reggie demonstrated such wondrous understanding.

THE NEXT MORNING she did not rise as early as she had planned, and so was not surprised to discover her brother well into his breakfast when she came down the stairs.

She turned her nose up at the steak and eggs upon his plate and settled for a small roll and cup of very hot tea.

"Are you feeling quite the thing, Lizzie?" he asked solicitiously. "You don't look terribly well."

"I didn't sleep well last night," she lied.

"Well, I do hope you feel better for your trip."

"Trip?" Lizzie shook the fog from her head and remembered belatedly. "Oh, yes, Valstry... I had forgotten. Is Valerie up?"

Lord Croyton raised an eyebrow and stole a closer look at his pale sister. His own memory was a well-known joke, but Lizzie never forgot a thing.

"I have no idea," he answered finally.

"Childers—" Lizzie caught the servant as he was leaving the dining room. "Miss Bach and I will be leaving shortly for Valstry. Could you see that Margaret knows to waken her?"

"I believe Miss Bach is already awake, My Lady," Childers replied with a bow. "Her woman took a tray upstairs a quarter of an hour ago, but I will relay your message."

Lizzie returned to her breakfast but found she had little appetite and decided instead to concentrate upon her tea.

She glanced up to find her brother regarding her quizzically.

"Not hungry?"

"No. Certainly not after looking at that." She waved at his plate. "How can you eat such so early in the morning?"

"Is it early? I rather thought it was later than usual. But I think that can be excused. Morning routine is often shattered by midnight jaunts."

Lizzie scoffed and sipped her tea as her brother's comment about morning routine jogged a memory. "Did you go riding?" she asked coyly.

The look of dismay on her brother's face was so comical that she laughed gaily.

"Oh, I know you do!" she proclaimed. "If the rest of London only knew! The very proper Lord Croyton up before eleven! Poor Aunt Martie would faint. You're up earlier than I am every morning and you ride for hours. Then you sneak back inside and pretend you've just got up. And there's not a servant in this house who, when asked, doesn't swear you're still abed. Such loyalty, Reggie!"

"Servants live for that sort of thing," declaimed the earl. "Secrets are their life's blood. And you must admit our life has, until recently, been devoid of interest. Must keep up appearances, what?"

She patted his hand. "Your secret's safe with me."

"If it's so safe," he looked doubtful, "why do you bring it up now?"

Lizzie set her cup down firmly and declared, "I want to know what happened last night between you and Costain."

"Nothing to tell, actually. I merely explained to Costain the likely outcome of any possible action he could take and he, being the sensible fellow he is, opted for the least violent."

"Then you *did* challenge him?" She leaned forward.

"Gad, no!" His eyes widened. "If I had, I seriously doubt I would be here now. But I had not forgotten my manners so much as not to give him an option. He could leave or he could stay, in either case, he would not have your friend. So he left. Simple."

IT'S FUN! IT'S FREE!
AND IT COULD MAKE YOU A
MILLIONAIRE

If you've ever played scratch-off lottery tickets, you should be familiar with how our games work. On each of the first four tickets (numbered 1 to 4 in the upper right)—there are PINK METALLIC STRIPS to scratch off.

Using a coin, do just that—carefully scratch the PINK STRIPS to reveal how much each ticket could be worth if it is a winning ticket. Tickets could be worth from $5.00 to $1,000,000.00 in lifetime money.

Note, also, that each of your 4 tickets has a unique sweepstakes Lucky Number...and that's 4 chances for a **BIG WIN!**

FREE BOOKS!

At the same time you play your tickets for big cash prizes, you are invited to play ticket #5 for the chance to get one or more free book(s) from Harlequin. We give away free book(s) to introduce readers to the benefits of the *Harlequin Reader Service*®.

Accepting the free book(s) places you under no obligation to buy anything! You may keep your free book(s) and return the accompanying statement marked "cancel". But if we don't hear from you, then every other month we'll deliver 4 of the newest Harlequin Regency™ novels right to your door. You'll pay the low members-only discount price of just $2.49* each—a savings of 26¢ apiece off the cover price. And there's no charge for shipping and handling!

Of course, you may play "THE BIG WIN" without requesting any free book(s) by scratching tickets #1 through #4 only. But remember, the first shipment of one or more books is FREE!

PLUS A FREE GIFT!

One more thing, when you accept the free book(s) on ticket #5 you are also entitled to play ticket #6 which is GOOD FOR A VALUABLE GIFT! Like the book(s) this gift is totally free and yours to keep as thanks for giving our Reader Service a try!

So scratch off the PINK STRIPS on all your BIG WIN tickets and send for everything today! You've got nothing to lose and everything to gain!

Lizzie's eyes gleamed appreciatively. "Do you think if you had fought him—"

His lordship raised a hand to forestall the question. "Too, too bloodthirsty of you, Lizzie! I shudder that you could even think such a thing."

"Yes," she sighed. "I hear he is good."

Lord Croyton elaborated with feeling. "The man is a crack shot and an even better swordsman. I have no desire to die so young, even for my pretty little sister."

"Well, I am certainly glad it's over," declared Lizzie. "I think I shall enjoy my stay in the country. I do so need a rest. Will you come up at all?"

He shook his head decisively. "I have done more travelling in the past two weeks than in the past two years. I shall stay in London."

Lizzie laughed and finished her tea.

Standing, she hesitated briefly before giving her brother a gentle hug. "Poor Reggie—" she kissed his forehead "—I do treat you so odiously. I wonder you put up with it."

His lordship casually patted the hand on his shoulder. "I always look to the future," he explained. "Someday, I may be in need of *your* assistance."

"You?" Lizzie exclaimed in mock disbelief. "My darling brother who will never 'just happen to fall in love?'" she teased.

"Much too brown, Lizzie."

"You will give me some clue I hope," the girl continued with a giggle, "before you go chasing through the night and duelling in public taverns. I would so hate to disgrace us both by fainting straightaway at the news."

"I have always condemned our late parent," the earl began, seemingly apropos of nothing, "for his lack of foresight, or anythin' resembling sensitivity. I must, however, admire his perception in the choice of your name.''

"Whatever do you mean?''

"Elizabeth is Hebrew—or somethin' like that. Translation: 'God's oath.'''

Lizzie bestowed a quick, graceful curtsy and a loving smile upon her sibling and practically skipped from the room.

Her light mood lasted well into the day.

CHAPTER TEN

SIR ANTONY SURVEYED the grounds of his ancestral home in anything but a light mood and kicked a stone down the dirt path leading from the mill to the great house.

It was a gloomy day in the county. Nature seemed to sense his mood and refrained from its usual springtime exuberance. The birds ceased their chatter and the green leaves of nearby trees rustled in muted voice. Clouds drifted overhead and blocked the sun's warmth, but the baronet did not pay any mind to the sudden chill.

It took less time to review the condition of his estate than he had envisaged. The house required considerable work, but its roof was sound and it was habitable—barely. A disquieting hollowness accompanied him as he walked through the halls and kicked up years of accumulated dust from threadbare carpets. A little furniture remained, not the best pieces, and even his ancestors' portraits had been sold, leaving vacant disapproving reminders against the paint.

He walked along a thin stretch of lush green pasture and through a stand of elms away from the rickety plank bridge over which the circuitous lane wound to its end before a large workshop. His great-grandfather had arranged the mill construction and it still remained the only paper mill in the county. It had produced well until his grandfather's day, but that gentleman acquired other, more sophisticated interests and these he passed on to his only son. The family trade and estate suffered considerably from the resultant neglect.

Sir Anthony remembered the mill only as a child's delightful playhouse, its true purpose long since forgotten. The fallen timbers offered a musty seclusion and protection against the vagaries of an adult world. Now, however, he looked upon the structure with adult eyes and saw only its failings.

Huge, iron-teethed stampers gaped in silent anticipation of the water and rags which had once fed them. The wooden bridge across a long stone vat was rotted and fallen and its splintered remains pointed an accusatory finger skyward, where gaps in the roof permitted entry to the rain and snow that had prompted its demise. Horsehair ropes, enmeshed in cobwebs, dangled from the rafters and swayed like gallows' nooses in the gentle breezes.

Ivy was everywhere in profusion. It hung upon the mill walls and latched itself to the unused waterwheel. Had it been possible to make paper from ivy, Sir Antony knew he should never have to worry for a steady supply.

He heard a stone skitter and bounce down the path.

"Can I help ye, sir?" a voice asked and immediately apologized. "Sorry to be startlin' ye, but ye look a bit lost."

The baronet turned to face the stranger.

A wizened old farmer squinted at him through watery eyes and breathed, "Lord! Sir Pat! God 'ave mercy. It be ye."

"I'm Antony Russelford," Sir Antony assured the frightened man quickly.

"Oh! Me poor 'eart," the man lamented and, as if questioning Sir Antony's veracity, stepped forward and examined him closely. "I told meself it couldna be he walkin' aboot the place, but me eyes ain't what they used to be. Ye've got the grand look o' Sir Pat aboot ye, ye do. Not many in these parts what remembers Sir Patrick, him what built the mill an' all.

"Name's Hokum, sir, Charlie Hokum. Was a vatman for yer grandpap afore the mill shut down. Be one of yer tenants now—little farm o'er the stream. Don' suppose ye be lost after all," Mr. Hokum surmised with a shrug.

"Actually, Mr. Hokum, I've never been more lost," he admitted.

"Well, if ye don' know where ye be—" the old man squinted dubiously "—I'm afraid I canna be much help to ye."

Sir Antony smiled. "I know where I am, Mr. Hokum, I just don't know where to go from here."

"Well now, that would depend on what ye be wantin'. Young man like yerself can't have too many worries. Less they be female problems," he added, winking playfully.

"A lady is just one of my problems, Mr. Hokum."

Mr. Hokum nodded with another appraising squint at the large man, and pronounced: "Women are a problem ye'll be havin' for the rest of yer life, I'll wager. Can't let 'em 'ave the upper 'and. Take me Emma for instance. I was a young fool thing and told 'er I loved 'er; wouldna have nothin' but that we get married. Then the mill shuts down and she was settled. 'Mr. Hokum,' she says to me, 'this here's me home an' I ain't movin'. An' if ye loves me like ye says, ye won't be leavin' me here to fend alone.' That's what she says so here I be, forty years o' farmin'."

"So what's your advice, Mr. Hokum—don't get married?"

"No, I loves me Emma, I do. She's been a fine wife to me, but I shouldna been so easy with 'er at first."

Sir Antony shoved his hands into his pockets and gazed back upon the mill.

Mr. Hokum coughed slightly after a few moments of silence and peered at the dilapidated building. "Pitiful shame it were when they shut down the mill," he said softly. "Ol' Sir Pat—meanin' no disrespect to his mem'ry, sir, 'Ol' Sir Pat' bein' what we called 'im— wouldna allowed it if 'e'd been livin'. No, sir! That mill was 'is life. Ye worked for yer keep and blast if he weren't right there workin' along wi' ye. An 'ard man, 'e were, but fair. Them was 'appy days. I seen ye down by the mill, sir," he continued, "ye be thinkin' aboot startin' 'er up agin?"

"No, Mr. Hokum," replied Sir Antony, "I haven't the blunt for it."

"Shame," the old man replied. "Got me a boy, taught 'im everythin' I knows. Got the 'stroke' he does, best damn vatman I've ever seen includin' myself. An' I was good in me day, I was." His hands spread apart to hold the invisible paper mould as he would have done if he had actually raised it from the heated vat of fibrous mulch. Swiftly, to illustrate his expertise, the farmer made a four-way combination sweeping, twisting motion of his arms and upper torso—the stroke. It was the start of life for every piece of paper.

"Ain't lost me touch." He smiled to himself. "An' me boy's just as good. 'Course, nowadays they got machines what does all the work. 'Ollendens, they's called."

"Hollanders," Sir Antony corrected.

"That's them," the former vatman agreed sagely. "No need for stampers no more. Just put the rags in one of those 'ollenders an' it chews 'em up good. Why they says, sir, that ye can even make the paper from plants; don' even need rags no more. Can ye believe such a thing? What will they be thinkin' up next?"

"Steam, Mr. Hokum, that's what they're thinking up next."

"Steam, sir?"

"Steam," he repeated and described to the old man all the glorious uses discovered for this exceptional energy source. "They have steam engines to fill the vats—no more waterwheels or bucket brigades. Steam to heat the water, run the hollanders, even—," he halted abruptly and ceased his abstracted pacing as an angry furrow beset his brow.

"Even?" prompted Mr. Hokum who had listened to the baronet's feverish tally of man's engineering progress with all the respect such accomplishments demanded, but remained superiorly content in the knowledge that such nonsense would never pass his doorstep unchallenged.

Sir Antony did not answer immediately, and Mr. Hokum was on the verge of rephrasing the question when he did. "Even work the press," he said dully.

"Pshaw!" spat the farmer. "No disrepect intended but—Blast! Where ye be off to?!"

"Soon they'll have machines that will do all the work," Sir Antony called over his shoulder as he marched purposefully back down the overgrown lane to the mill.

He trampled through the ivy and ripped it from the mill walls. Mr. Hokum panted as he followed in the wake of Sir Antony's frantic destruction.

"Where's the press?"

"Agin that far wall," the farmer answered, and barely caught the coat flung at him from across the floor.

"They have machines, Mr. Hokum," bellowed Sir Antony, "that heat water and run hollanders and they can probably make paper out of ivy but they still need all hands to the press!''

In the corner, he uncovered the mammoth machine. The garagantuan press, requiring the strength of many workers to expel excess water from the paper fibres, stood immune to the ravages of time. Ivy tendrils clung to its side till it was indistinguishable from the mill wall, but failed to implant themselves within the sturdy timbers of its frame.

"Ye be wantin' yer coat?" Mr. Hokum wiped his forehead and lowered himself upon a nearby bench.

"What I want, Mr. Hokum, is a sickle, a hammer, an anvil and whatever spare pieces of metal you can find," responded the baronet as he removed the excess foliage. "And I passed a tannery on the road..."

"Aye, that be Pete Gert's place. Ye be wantin' that, too?"

"No, but he has a smithy there and a couple of good boilers."

"Them ol' kilns," spat Mr. Hokum, "ain't worth nothin'."

"Then he won't object to parting with them, will he?" countered Sir Antony with a smile.

"No. Doubt 'e will."

Mr. Hokum watched patiently from his perch as the baronet, barehanded and now stripped to shirt sleeves, dug out around and behind the huge piece of equipment. Rotted boards, weeds and discarded refuse of all kinds flew across the enclosure to land in a pile by the vats.

After a quarter of an hour at this wearisome pastime, the farmer stood and deposited Sir Antony's coat carefully upon his seat. He added his own and with a skyward glance of reproach, accused bitterly, "Couldna let a man rest in his old age, now could ye?"

Mr. Hokum was granted a slight respite only three hours later as, returned to his bench, he etched numbers into a small board.

"And what good does this do ye?" he asked as Sir Antony ceased his methodical toe-to-toe measure of the entire mill floor and finally came to a rest beside him.

"It tells me, Mr. Hokum—" Sir Antony accepted the board and reviewed the figures, making his own small notations at the sides "—that I have enough space to place those two boilers Mr. Gert will be kind enough to supply me between the water feed to the stampers and the press and still leave room for a runoff to the vats."

"It will, will it?" The farmer peered over Sir Antony's shoulder dubiously.

"That one section of roof is almost nonexistent," he continued thinking aloud. "Inconvenient but not impossible to work around so long as the rafters are sound and the good weather lasts. I'd best get up there later to have a see. And those stampers will need to be replaced shortly. Even if they work now, they're simply too antiquated to keep.

"The vats are in good shape, surprisingly. I'd like a better look at them, though, before deciding." He stood up abruptly. "Come, sir, let's clear the wreckage!"

"And when we've done that?" queried Mr. Hokum as he climbed painfully down to the ground.

"Then to the waterwheel. I must know what condition it's in."

"And when we've done *that*?"

"Then we see Mr. Gert and begin building our new press. And if it works, Mr. Hokum, if it works, then I'll have a brand-new kind of paper mill to sell. That ought to be worth something.''

"And then?'' Mr. Hokum shook his head wearily.

"And then, Mr. Hokum,'' Sir Antony summed up his plans with a laugh, "I shall need a good vatman.''

"Now I'm understandin' ye! Yer startin' her up agin!''

"Yes, Mr. Hokum, I am starting her up again. Are you with me?''

"Aye!'' exclaimed the farmer and he gleefully tossed a fallen board upon the immense refuse pile, only to stop short and glance suspiciously at the younger man. "So long as ye be rememberin','' he cautioned, "that there ain't no machine what can replace a good vatman.''

"Not yet,'' agreed Sir Antony with a twinkle in his eye.

"Not ever,'' replied Mr. Hokum adamantly.

THE FARMER'S CENSURE aside, his assistance and an amenable Mr. Gert proved invaluable over the next few days. The long hours of exacting physical labour cleared Sir Antony's mind and proved that his makeshift design would work, and he departed for London in less than a week with plans for his new mill tucked securely in his right breast pocket.

He prepared to find someone with enough capital to finance the entire renovation project. This mythical soul, Sir Antony thought, laughing at his own foolhardiness, would need to possess the generosity of a saint, for he couldn't mind waiting five years or more for a return on his investment.

It was to Mr. Gentry that Sir Antony first presented himself upon his arrival in London.

"You want to do what?'' the old man choked out.

"It will work, sir,'' he proclaimed. "The mill can be renovated and adapted to work. I'll use the stampers at the start to defray costs, and then convert to hollanders. Everything is still there, not in the best of shape, of course, and I will have to replace the press eventually, but I already have the name of a good vatman.''

Sir Antony explained his idea for the third time, but his tone rang as bright as it had the first.

''But, my dear boy—'' the lawyer shook his head again ''—you have no idea of the cost involved.''

''I have a very good idea, sir, and I know it is more than I can afford. I shall require an investment partner. He supplies the money and I do the work.''

''But, my dear boy...''

''I realize that I put it too simply and it will not be easy finding someone interested, but if you could see yourself clear to give me a little advice I would be most appreciative. Point me in the right direction, sir, and I'll give it a go.''

''My dear boy...'' Realizing that he had only been repeating himself for the past hour, Mr. Gentry coughed self-consciously. ''You've had something of a shock since your return,'' he began again. ''Your position has worsened but what you plan is not sane. Consider your alternatives, I beg of you.''

Sir Antony shook his head. ''My only alternative is to sell the land outright and take what I can get for it. You yourself said it would not be much. I will not do so, at any rate. You asked me to visit the place before I made any decision. I have done so as a favour to you. Will you not, sir, return the favour?''

The old man looked upon the hard set of Sir Antony's jaw and the unwavering gaze of his clear blue eyes. This was not the same man he had interviewed in his offices five days earlier.

''What is it you want from me again?'' he sighed.

If Sir Antony felt triumph, he did not show it. "I shall need to review the books more closely, and I would appreciate your assistance with the accounts until such time as I am able to take them over."

Mr. Gentry nodded.

"I shall need the services of a reputable engineer and I believe your firm has upon occasion been wont to use one. I have an idea how to proceed but I lack the experience and training.

"Also, as you have yourself noted, I lack sufficient capital to implement the renovation. I thought perhaps you might be able to give me an idea of where I should begin to look for a partner."

"I'm afraid that will be the most difficult task ahead of you," the lawyer declared, confirming Sir Antony's own fears. "I would begin with the firm of Jeffries and Jeffries. They handle several large accounts. Although most of their clients invest in more established businesses, you might just be lucky enough to find someone willing to give a chance to the underdog. I don't have much hope for you," he said, "but I've known Calvin Jeffries for years. If you like, I can make enquiries for you."

The baronet smiled warmly. "I would appreciate that, sir."

Gentry was not finished and warned, "You know the only collateral you have is the land itself. You could lose everything and end in debtor's prison, as well. I couldn't help you there."

"I could lose everything anyway, and as far as debtor's prison is concerned—it would at least be a roof over my head," Sir Antony replied wryly.

The feeble jest passed unheeded. "You might consider some of your old friends," pondered Mr. Gentry.

"Although that often leads to more trouble than it's worth, but I understand several of them are quite wealthy. Lord Croyton, for instance?"

Sir Antony shook his head abruptly. "No. I could never ask his lordship. I might give some others a try if I have to. Lord Graneville was a good friend of Father's and I know him from my youth. Also, I remember Father mentioning once that he gave George Bach his start."

Gentry shook his head. "Maybe true, maybe not. One never knew with Sir Geoffrey. I remember having to take things with a pinch of salt. Don't be disappointed if Bach tells a different story. He's a businessman though—to the core. If anyone can convince you of the foolishness of your scheme, he can. Doesn't mince words, from what I hear. By all means, lad, go see the man. Then come back to me and we'll see what other schemes we can devise."

"I know you mean well, so I won't be disheartened by your lack of faith," Sir Antony said, laughing goodnaturedly and shaking the older man's hand. "You will let me know about the other items."

Mr. Gentry nodded. "I'll do what I can for you, my boy. Good luck."

Sir Antony left Brown, Haverstock and Gentry feeling anything but light-hearted. To convince Mr. Gentry his plan was feasible was only the first step and certainly not the most difficult to its implementation.

After a few quick questions and a short walk, he confronted Geroge Bach's private secretary. His heart pounded in his chest as he watched his card disappear into a ghostly white palm and the owner of the palm vanish behind an ostentatiously ornate door. Wondering if he hadn't committed some unforgivable breach of etiquette, Sir Antony paced before the secretary's desk, and panic struck as he realized that he had no idea what he was going to say.

CHAPTER ELEVEN

MR. BIDDLE STOOD respectfully beside his employer's desk. It was never a good idea to disturb Mr. Bach when he read. At last, the magnate turned his restless eyes upon his secretary.

"Yes?" he demanded brusquely.

"A gentleman to see you, sir," replied Mr. Biddle as he presented Sir Antony's card.

"Russelford?" Mr. Bach frowned. "Russelford? Where have I heard that name? What's this fellow look like?"

"A fine-looking young man, if I may say so, about twenty-five years of age, sir."

"Bah! Send him away!" He tossed the card back in disgust. "You know I don't see anyone this time of day, Biddle. What's got into you?"

Mr. Biddle coughed hesitantly. "He says, sir, that you knew his father, Sir Geoffrey."

Mr. Bach's head came up with a start. "Sir Geoffrey?! Good Lord! Well, don't just stand there! Send the boy in!"

Sir Antony had almost completely given up hope when the magnificent door opened wide and he was ushered through. There was no time to take stock of his surroundings as a firm hand gripped his and a pair of keen, birdlike eyes flitted over him. In a minute, he felt as if he had been measured faster and better than any tailor could have done.

"So you're Sir Geoffrey's cub." It was a comment, not a question. "Well, you don't take after him."

Sir Antony wasn't certain if this was a compliment, so he merely nodded.

"Sit down. Sit down."

The large room was a business man's office where little artifice or grandeur existed. The desk commanded all attention but even it was no larger than necessary and appeared well used. Overstocked bookshelves and an escritoire were, aside from the chairs, the only other furnishings. The office was hardly empty, however, for the presence of the man seated across the desk from Sir Antony permeated every corner.

Mr. Bach leaned back in his chair and contemplated his fingers. "I saw Sir Geoffrey for the last time more than thirty years ago. I was sorry when he died." This sentimental vein did not endure, and with a sharpness that took Sir Antony's breath away, he demanded, "What is it you want?"

"Sir?"

"Come, come. You're here for a reason, lad. Spit it out!"

"I'm here, sir, to discuss a business proposition." Sir Antony surprised himself with the sureness of his tone, and with no unnecessary elaboration, he laid out the facts of his situation, the condition of his estate and the solution he had devised. He hoped desperately that he sounded reasonably intelligent, but the expression on the businessman's face did not alter.

"So," began Mr. Bach as Sir Antony concluded his proposal, "you expect me to sink my money into this cock-and-bull scheme simply because I knew your father."

"No, sir, I do not. I freely admit that I used the acquaintance as a means to get in to see you. You have my apologies. Desperate men are apt to do desperate things, I'm afraid. I fully expected to be ejected from your office long before this." He smiled wanly. "I respectfully request that you judge myself and my proposition strictly upon our own merits without regard to past associations."

George Bach smiled slightly. "You don't take after him, so I won't hold the relationship against you."

Once again nonplussed by the other man's remarks, Sir Antony ventured hesitantly, "He never discussed details, but he did mention once that he gave you your start."

"Gave me my start!" The portly man popped out of his chair like cannon shot. "Damn the man's hide!" He bellowed several more none too kind commentaries upon Sir Geoffrey's memory and began to pace furiously, only to stop suddenly and let out another raucous cry. "If there ever existed such a complete jackanapes!"

"That is enough!" Sir Antony stood outraged. "You speak quite freely about a man not able to defend himself, sir. You forget that he was my father and any differences you may have had aside, he was a good man."

"A good man doesn't leave his son begging for money," countered Mr. Bach.

The baronet's jaw tightened. "A good man, sir, uses what he has to the best of his ability—without complaint. That may or may not make him successful in the eyes of the world. I apologize again for my intrusion. Good day."

"I suppose—" Mr. Bach interrupted Sir Antony's angry departure "—to give credit where credit is due, he did give me a push in the right direction."

He shook his head, rocked on the balls of his feet and shrugged. "Fell in love with the same girl, we did," he explained. "Some chit out of the schoolroom—not that it mattered; we both married someone else. Buried myself in my father's trade to ease my aching heart. Found out I enjoyed the work and was damn good at it. The rest is history."

He returned to the present abruptly. "I've listened to what you've said, lad, and you make a fine case. Waste of equipment just sitting there, and your ideas are sound. This is the age for new ideas, experiments, machinery— that's the future. Learn, implement and relearn—best things a man can do to survive.

"I suggest you contact a fellow named Jason Rory— best damn steam man I know. Biddle can give you his address."

"Then you're in, sir?"

Mr. Bach shook his head. "I'm a shipper, sir, made my money in trade and on the Exchange. I invest in solidity—the land is the only thing destined to survive us all. What would I do with a decrepit paper mill except pour good money into it? The only item of value you possess is the land itself."

"Which I am quite prepared to offer as collateral," pursued Sir Antony.

With another shake of his head, Mr. Bach responded as gently as he could. "Damn sight too risky even for *my* blood. Take the advice of a veteran, son, and sell the property outright. It'll hurt less."

"Thank you for your time and the advice but I will never sell without trying."

"A good businessman never says never. And he never—" Mr. Bach grinned at his joke "—buys a pig in a poke. I'll think it over, but I guarantee nothing."

"Thank you, sir."

Sir Antony returned to his quiet apartments and the notion seized him that an afternoon spent in those dreary lodgings was certain to drive him mad.

He craved companionship and changed quickly into nankeen breeches, white stockings and a blue-and-gold brocade waistcoat. His smart double-breasted tailcoat possessed a rounded collar and the points and cut were horridly outdated, but the dark broadcloth had worn well and did not show its age. He tied his cravat simply and in a style he considered quite pleasing to the eye.

Never one to give much thought to his appearance, he examined his reflection carefully. There was no denying that his wardrobe was antiquated but he could hardly afford a new one.

He shrugged into his caped greatcoat and picked up a small timepiece, smiled fondly and placed it in his waistcoat pocket. It had been a gift from Lizzie and he never went anywhere without it. Other than the small signet ring on his right hand, it was his only ornament.

Sir Antony headed for White's and found that the balmy night had brought out more than the usual number of members. Those who could not find—or did not want—seats lined the walls or milled about, engaging in and leaving conversations with nonchalant carelessness. Whether they were present for the camaraderie, the gossip, the liquor, the games of chance or simply to boast of their latest coat from Weston did not matter. The hectic result would have been the same.

Sir Antony wandered aimlessly and answered innumerable questions about the state of affairs in Jamaica, the people and the styles, and after each conversation, walked away with the sinking feeling that perhaps he should have visited a tailor before breaching the halls of Society. He chided himself for his paranoia and awoke at the faro tables.

There, in regal splendour, sat Lord Croyton.

Across from him, in equal—if less colourful—splendour, was Martin Costain. The latter was dressed entirely in black, save for cuffs and cravat, the only splash of colour in his attire a single silver fob chain in his waistcoat. The suit of dittos proved singularly striking combined with Costain's dark hair and features.

"Devilish fellow," Sir Antony heard another newcomer whisper and he agreed heartily.

Costain's very attitude reeked of condescension, from the arrogant curl of his lip to the exaggerated manner in which he placed his bets. He played deep, and despite reckless betting essayed a sizeable win, drinking deeper with each new success. Two glasses of port disappeared in the short time since the baronet's entry.

As he approached the game, Sir Antony waded into the tension between the two men at the table. Costain made each wager as though it were a challenge, lounging back and gazing at his opponent triumphantly while a malevolent hint of a grin, which contained no mirth and did not touch his eyes, twisted his lips. The wine alone could not be responsible for the wicked gleam he directed at the earl.

Lord Croyton placed his bets quietly, judiciously and with little emotion, and gave no indication that he noticed the condition of his fellow gamester. The glass at his elbow sat untouched through the duration of play.

It was not until the end of the game that a word was exchanged between the two men.

Lord Croyton stood, retrieved his glass and bowed in Costain's direction. "Congratulations, dear fellow," he said. "It seems your luck has changed. You've come away a winner."

"This time," acknowledged Costain.

Though slightly dulled by the wine, his words stopped the earl in midturn and contained a message that was obvious to all. "Tell me, Lord Croyton," he asked, "how is your beautiful sister?"

Sir Antony moved forward as the crowd hushed and Lord Croyton returned a perplexed "Lizzie? She's quite well, thank you. I'll tell her you enquired."

"Please do." Costain smiled in overt friendliness and his eyes sparkled. "I was particularly concerned that she appeared rather pale when last we met. I suppose it was the circumstances."

"No doubt," his lordship replied noncommittally and twirled his eyeglass absently.

Costain's smile grew broader and his eyes invited the crowd around them into his secret. In a voice like silk, he continued, "You know what they say about combining night air and long—" he paused significantly for the benefit of the assembled "—northern journeys."

All eyes focussed upon the bland features of Lord Reginald Croyton, perhaps the most innocuous patron of White's, suddenly thrust into the foreground of controversy. What secret existed between the two men not even the most omniscient gossip knew and an eternity seemed to pass before the earl responded.

"I have heard," he remarked, "something to that effect. But I have never found it to be the case. I have always thought the night air to be particularly refreshin' and journeyin' at night quite peaceful. That way one avoids the ordinary traffic, what?

"As a matter of fact, one meets some of the most interestin' people travellin' at night. Why just the other
day—or night, rather—I was returnin' from Bristol
and—"

"I see it was foolish of me to be concerned, but—"

"Excuse me, Sir," interjected Sir Antony, placing a
hand on his friend's elbow. "Reggie, I must speak to
you."

"Tony! This is a pleasure! When did you get in?!"

Sir Antony noted Costain's dark scowl as he slipped
into the crowd and ordinary banter returned to the room.

"Let me look at you," commanded Lord Croyton, and
he stepped away and trained a critical eye upon the baronet.

Under the earl's proprietary gaze, Sir Antony doubly
felt the inadequacy of his attire and the change in his
friend's expression from pleasure to marked distaste only
heightened his discomfiture.

"My dear fellow," his lordship demanded, "where did
you get those clothes?"

Sir Antony attempted a lame grin. "Obviously not at
the same place you get yours," he answered and indicated the earl's cleanly tapered coat with its high stand-
fall collar which successfully prohibited abrupt movement. A yellow-and-lavender striped waistcoat topped his
buckskin breeches squarely and his lace starcher was tied
with superb intricacy. Lord Croyton was dressed in the
height of fashionable excess.

"I should hope not," he stated unequivocally, "or I
shall have to take my trade elsewhere."

"I do need to speak to you, Reggie," Sir Antony repeated. "Someplace a little more private."

His lordship peered sideways. "Dash it!" he exclaimed, managing to sound not in the least perturbed.

"Where did the fellow run off to? I forgot to thank him for his concern. Oh, well—" he sighed "—have you eaten?"

"No."

His lordship brightened. "Capital, neither have I. Shall we?"

It was several minutes before the two gentlemen found a secluded table and were able to enjoy their repast and each other's company.

The two old friends had much to discuss, so they might have been excused if it required considerable time to review their respective healths, Sir Antony's trip, current events in the world and styles and fashions. Lord Croyton proved particularly concerned over the latter category and his friend's callous disregard for it.

"My dear fellow," he cried plaintively, "you really must do something about your wardrobe. It positively grieves me to look at what you have on. Sink me, if you're not at least three years behind the times. Don't they have tailors in the Americas?"

"Yes, they have tailors," replied Sir Antony with a laugh. "But a person needs money to pay them for their handiwork."

"That bad? In that case, I don't believe I'll recommend my fellow, after all. Pity, he does do excellent work. But I'm afraid he is gettin' a tad dear even for my tastes."

His lordship emphasized this point with a quick flick of his wrist and the lace cuff flew backward. Twirling his wineglass between long, well-manicured fingers, he straightened the errant cloth expertly.

Sir Antony watched the earl's display uneasily and cleared his throat. "I'm afraid I'm going to have to struggle along with what I have for a little while longer,'' he said.

Lord Croyton raised a questioning eyebrow and returned his friend's smile with an insipid grin. ''Pray allow me to show you the latest style someday. That way at least, I'll have somethin' decent to look at.''

''If you insist,'' the baronet shrugged.

The reply was fervently insistent. ''Oh, I do! Most certainly, I do.''

Sir Antony laughed with a heartiness he was far from feeling. ''It is good to see you again, Reggie.''

The object of this declaration blinked. ''Well, I should hope so,'' he breathed. ''Did you think it might not be?''

''No, no.'' Laughter died quickly on Sir Antony's lips as he pushed his plate aside and met the pair of pale, bored eyes directly. ''What was all that downstairs?'' he asked.

The veiled eyes did not waver. ''The faro tables, dear boy. You've seen them before.''

''You know what I mean. With Costain.''

''The fellow was drunk and feeling quite pleased with himself for finally having won.''

''There was more to it than that. The comments he made about Lizzie were direct enough. Even you couldn't have missed their meaning. Why does Costain want you to call him out?''

The battle of wills ended, for Lord Croyton blinked and smiled. ''Really, Tony,'' he complained, ''you're gone for more than two years and all we can find to talk about is the inconsequential blitherings of a drunkard. The fellow was in his cups, hardly worth more than passing interest, if that. Tell me, what are your plans now that you're back among the livin'?''

Sir Antony sat back. He recognized his friend's obvious evasiveness as the earl's tactful way of instructing him to mind his own affairs. He was unaccustomed to the estrangement and replied flatly; "Renovation of Brentshire."

"Ah, yes, I do recall Lizzie mentioning something about the place. Now, what was it? Blast this memory of mine."

"I told her I was going out there and that I would see you when I returned," the baronet supplied.

"That must be it, then." His lordship sipped his wine and after a moment's pause, asked pleasantly, "You found everything in order, I trust?"

The answer was a snort.

"I wouldn't want to burden you with my problems, Reggie," Sir Antony added harshly. "You obviously have some of your own."

"Yes, most tiring," sighed the other. "I'm not at all pleased with the new snuff I bought. I really must stop trying these new blends. They're always so disagreeable. And I cannot tell you how many times I've sent this coat back—blasted thing pinches something monstrous. Most tiring," he repeated.

Sir Antony stared at his companion. Reggie had always been on the dull side and slightly particular about certain things. That had not changed over the years, but the man now appeared to be a member of the dandy set— a regular fop! All he thought about was nonsense. If three years could change a man so horridly, how much had he himself changed? He prayed that it was for the better. At length he roused himself from this introspection under the watchful gaze of Lord Croyton.

"I say, old chap, are you feeling quite the thing?" the earl asked.

Sir Antony shook his head. "I'm sorry, Reggie. I'm afraid I wasn't paying attention. My fault. What were you saying?"

"Quite all right." He waved the apology aside. "Can't say I understand the reaction, but I am getting quite used to it."

Sir Antony grinned apologetically and changed the subject. "You haven't told me, how are things with you and Lizzie?"

"Didn't she tell you when you saw her?"

"We had a bit of a falling out."

His lordship nodded as if this were sufficient explanation. "We're quite well," he stated, "but then Lizzie's always well. Never sick a day in her life—marvellous constitution. Just like my father, never a moment's complaint, then—" he snapped his fingers. "Well, you remember."

The wine in his glass seemed to hold a particular fascination for Sir Antony and it was some time before he ventured to ask his next question. "I wonder...do you think...she would see me?"

"Dashed awkward at the moment, I'm afraid. You see, she's not in London," the earl replied casually.

Sir Antony glanced up as Costain's words echoed in his head, and a picture of a letter dropping to the floor came vividly to mind.

Lord Croyton must not have noticed his tight-lipped expression for he continued in the same lighthearted vein. "Gone over to Valstry with a friend," he said. "Been gone nearly a week now."

"With a friend?" repeated Sir Antony doubtfully.

"Yes, met in school or some such thing—not quite sure meself. Lizzie never tells me anything, but then, come to think on it, no one else ever tells me anything, either. No matter, I'm certain you can see her when she returns."

Sir Antony condemned his temper. What right had he to be angry? What Lizzie did was not his concern. He had no claim on her; he had foolishly seen to that.

"When will she return?" he asked.

Lord Croyton frowned. "Oh, a month, maybe less."

He was tempted to ask if Lizzie had mentioned their meetings but decided against it. The more he saw of his friend, the more unlikely it seemed and Reggie had just said that Lizzie never confided in him.

"I suppose it can wait," he muttered. "I have a great deal of business which will keep me occupied."

"You must come to dinner some night," invited his lordship. "With Lizzie away, I shall be deuced put out to keep meself entertained."

Sir Antony smiled noncommittally.

"Same old cook, so the food will be barely palatable—" the earl grinned "—but I can guarantee the best port in town. Say—next Thursday?"

"Next Thursday. Just like old times?"

"Exactly!"

"Just like old times" was impossible, the baronet realized, and his unease increased as his eyes dropped beneath the warm gaze of his old comrade. He coughed abruptly. "You'll have to excuse me. I'm afraid I'll have to make it an early evening. I have a busy day tomorrow.

"It was good to see you again, Reggie," he repeated as they shook hands.

"The proverbial sight for sore eyes, what?"

Sir Antony's feeling of awkwardness soared unbearably when the grip on his hand tightened and he stared into a set of cool blue eyes as the earl, his voice lacking all trace of affectation, advised, "If there is anything you need, Tony, just ask.'' Then the eyes clouded and focussed upon a point just beyond the baronet's right shoulder. ''Remember, I am your friend,'' added his lordship glibly.

Sir Antony could not be certain during his walk home if he had thanked his friend for the offer or if, in fact, there had *been* an offer, so abrupt was the transition. He knew only that he left White's with far more questons than answers.

CHAPTER TWELVE

"A WORD WITH YOU, young man."

Lady Graneville swept into the library without waiting to be announced.

Startled, Lord Croyton looked up from the pile of papers before him but smiled fondly. "And hello to you, too, Aunt Martie."

Her ladyship nodded briskly and removed her kid gloves and wide-brimmed bonnet. Her stern expression did not alter. "It is time, sir, for a serious discussion with regard to your sister's behaviour and her future," she pronounced and, training a jaundiced eye upon his lordship, added, "not to mention yours."

Rounding the side of the desk, the earl responded blandly to the onslaught. "You're looking particularly fetching today, dear Aunt. The dress is new, isn't it? The colour becomes you."

Lady Graneville could not resist a smile at the compliment. "Thank you, m'dear. It's the latest thing," she said and turned to allow the earl a full view of the light green overskirt. "Do you like it? Ordinarily, I don't like to pay so much attention to the new fashions. One can quite easily become conceited, you know. This time, however, I was particularly enchant—"

Realizing that she had been distracted from her purpose, she laughed scoldingly. "Oh! Come give your aunt a kiss, dear boy. Imagine, keeping me waiting so!"

Lord Croyton obeyed the directive promptly.

"I've instructed Childers to serve us tea here," she said as he bussed her cheek. She seated herself confidently.

"But I don't drink—"

"But I do! What can have happened to your manners? Sit down."

Lady Graneville scrutinized the earl's inexpressive face and shook her head.

"How was your trip?" she asked.

"Trip?"

"Bristol."

"Oh, yes," he said with a nod. "It was relatively uneventful, except for the return. First night out I was stopped by perhaps the most congenial highway—"

"Where's Lizzie?" she interrupted brusquely.

His lordship blinked. "Valstry. As I was saying—"

"What the devil is she doing at Valstry?"

"Haven't the faintest. What does *anyone* do in the country?"

"There are so many excellent activities one can find to do. Excellent riding, hunting, fishing..." She shook her head again, for she did not approve of being distracted and certainly not twice in one interview. "Well, I'm pleased to see that you've come to your senses and got the girl out of town, at least," she judged. "I was never more shocked when I heard the latest."

"Latest?"

"Antony Russelford has returned!" she announced and leaned back on the settee to observe the result of her shattering news.

"And?"

"I know he was a good friend of yours, Reggie," she continued, covering her dismay expertly, "but he was never suitable husband material. Now he's returned and is making himself particularly disagreeable. Almost every person I know has been accosted by him."

"Never thought of Tony as the violent type," he responded.

"Looking for money, he is!" exclaimed her ladyship. "Some silly scheme to put the mill at Brentshire to work. Imagine that—it hasn't been operating since his grandfather's day! The poor lad is demented." Her voice lowered slightly and she confided, "Do you realize he actually asked Henry—my Henry!—for money? Put the touch on everyone of any consequence. It's frightful!"

The arrival of tea prevented the earl from replying to the good lady's remarks. He watched her pour with a visible shudder but accepted passively the offered cup.

"Drink your tea," she commanded. "It's good for you."

Confident that her words would be obeyed, Lady Graneville picked up her conversation where she had left it. "You can't tell me you haven't heard, or that he hasn't approached you!"

"Oh, I've heard," agreed the earl after a brief pause. "I believe somebody was mentioning it just yesterday at White's...or was it Boodle's? Come to think of it, I don't believe it was yesterday... perhaps the day before?"

"There's no end to the talk. But does it concern him? I should say not! As confident as you please, he walks about without the slightest regard for sensibilities. Imagine flaunting one's poverty so! It's most disgraceful." She closed the discussion with a thankful sigh. "Well, you've got that silly girl out of danger, that's a relief! She'd probably run off with him the moment he asked and then he'd have his money and where would we be? Which brings me to the subject of my visit. It's time you took some action."

"Yes, I see it is," he concurred quietly.

"Now, I realize this may be difficult for you to understand or accept, Reggie, but Lizzie is no longer a young girl. The moment has come for a decision." She took a deep breath and continued, "I've given the matter a great deal of thought because I love the child dearly and wouldn't wish her unhappy. I believe our best choice is Mr. Markham. Not a charmer, of course, but certainly a very steady gentleman. *Reggie!* Are you listening to me?"

Her sharp words brought him out of his reverie. "Um? Yes, Mr. Markham."

"It's true," she allowed, "that he's a bit older than Lizzie, but I don't think that's necessarily a disadvantage. He'll have a firmer hand on the reins, so to speak. After all, you must admit Lizzie does need discipline in her life. You haven't been able to supply it. I think her husband should most decidedly be of a more determined mien.

"You're a sweet boy, Reggie—" she smiled at him lovingly "—and I know you mean well, but I don't believe you have any conception of how awkward your sister's situation is becoming. She's refused every proposal that's come her way; her behaviour is becoming more outlandish every year, and she's getting older!"

"We all are."

"Soon—" she ignored him "—no decent man in his right mind will want to marry her. She'll be the object of attentions from all manner of fortune hunters and toadies. It's begun already. Why, she's even taken up with Martin Costain, of all people! So you can imagine how serious this matter may become if something isn't done promptly."

Lady Graneville rested for a moment, then chided the young man softly. "Whether through ignorance or lethargy—it isn't important which—you, sir, have condoned her actions. It may be too late to repair the damage completely, but I think you should speak to Lizzie about Mr. Markham. A little encouragement from her is all he needs. I'm certain of it.''

''Mr. Markham is a bore.''

''Reggie!''

He waved his hand with a frown. ''She'd drive the poor man mad within a fortnight.''

''I think they would be very well suited. But,'' she conceded after weighing his judgement, ''if you have a better suggestion, I'm willing to hear it.''

''No, nothing better at the moment,'' sighed Lord Croyton. ''Need some time to think on it.''

''Just don't take too long. You do agree with me that Lizzie should be married and that it is your responsibility to bring the subject up to her?'' She accepted his silence as agreement and proceeded, ''Now then, it has come to my attention that your conduct has been lacking in the observance of certain proprieties.''

''It has?'' his lordship queried, obviously pleased by her euphemisms.

''Yes, it has.'' Her ladyship frowned. ''How do you imagine, young man, that you can go about telling girls questionable tales? Even if the girl is your sister. There wasn't a thing I could tell her about Martin Costain she didn't already know. Learned from you, I understand. Such tales are not meant for female ears!''

''In that case, dear Aunt, how is it you know them?'' His eyes twinkled.

''I am a married woman, sir,'' she replied, piqued. ''It's a different matter entirely.''

Lord Croyton placed his untouched cup of tea upon the table and stood. ''And when you've married Lizzie off to Mr. Markham, then *she* will be a married woman and it will be a different matter entirely. Correct?''

Lady Graneville suppressed her laugh. There was no arguing with the boy's insane logic. ''Oh, very well,'' she granted. ''No harm done, I suppose. Just do be careful, Reggie. A man in your position cannot be too careful.''

''My position?''

''Rich, titled, young and—'' she hesitated ''—handsome.''

''Thank you.''

''You're a catch, dear boy,'' she admonished. ''Women will set their snares for you. You must watch every word you say. Unless...''

''Unless?''

Satisfied that she at last had his full attention, Lady Graneville snatched another deep breath and broached the third and final reason for her visit. ''Now that we've reached a decision about Lizzie,'' she said, ''let us move on to you.''

''Me?''

''How old are you?'' she asked pointedly.

''Don't you remember?'' he countered blankly.

''You're twenty-five. How long do you propose to wait? Till you're thirty? That's much too late. You, sir, have a lineage to consider.''

His eyes widened. ''Don't tell me, you've discovered just the suitable person to put some discipline into *my* life?'' he moaned.

''As a matter of fact—''

''M'dear Aunt Martie,'' he interrupted briskly and not without a trace of reproach, ''I allow you to say what you will about Lizzie because I happen to agree with you. It's time she was married. I do not, however, agree with a similar assessment of my own situation. Before you say anything we might both regret, pray give the matter more thought. Believe me, unless I die tomorrow—in which case the point is purely academic—I have no intention of leaving this earth without an heir. I do, though, insist upon pickin' my own partner in the venture.''

Surprised at his sudden vehemence, Lady Graneville stammered, ''I—I had no idea you would feel so...so strongly. Very well, Reggie, I'll say no more on the subject.''

An awkward silence passed between them until Lord Croyton cleared his throat and frowned. ''I wonder, Aunt Martie,'' he began, ''just for curiosity's sake, you realize, you mentioned you had someone in mind...?''

The earl later marvelled at his own endurance as he found himself subsequently subjected to a two-hour discourse upon the numerous attributes of various fine ladies whom Lady Graneville considered worthy of his attention. Only after vetoing the lot for what he considered variously fine reasons and offending his aunt for the second time that day, did he assume the mantle of responsibility which events so ungraciously shoved upon him.

AT PRECISELY four o'clock, Lord Croyton presented his card to a little man behind a desk and announced, ''Kindly inform Mr. Bach that I await his pleasure.''

Mr. Biddle, though unaccustomed to receiving such company, did not permit the earl's grand attire nor his disdainful expression to disconcert him. Quality did not habitually call upon Mr. Bach, much less await his pleasure.

He retired into the inner office and, as he expected, was instructed to show the gentleman in without delay.

"I appreciate your seeing me," Lord Croyton stated and summarily dispensed with all the usual pleasantries. "I can understand how busy you must be, so I shan't keep you long."

"As long as you need, my lord," Mr. Bach contradicted his normally abrupt behaviour in view of his visitor's social position.

The earl read his thoughts. "You're no doubt wondering what the devil I'm doin' here."

"I am."

Lord Croyton smiled apologetically. "I do not approve of involving oneself unnecessarily in another's affairs," he said. "Such behaviour is degrading—not to mention exhausting. I act when driven to it and I despise myself for the weakness. Would you describe that as a good attitude for a successful man of trade?"

"No, I would not," the magnate answered honestly, then demanded, "Are you interested in business, my lord?"

"Not particularly," said his lordship evasively. "I have a friend, however, who's quite set on revitalizing an old paper mill—"

"Sir Antony?"

"You've met him?"

"He visited me last week."

"Then you're familiar with his plans?"

"I am," answered Mr. Bach with a cough. He had given no more thought to the young baronet's schemes and did not enjoy discovering himself in the uncomfortable position of justifying his decision to a man who confessed himself uninterested in business matters. To offend the earl would be undiplomatic, especially as the peer's sister had graciously taken his daughter under her wing, but Mr. Bach would not be pinned by such delicacies. He was first and foremost a man of business and his lordship had seen fit to visit him within his own domain.

"There are a number of reasons why I was obliged to refuse your friend," he explained. "To name a few—"

"Sir Antony lacks experience," interjected Lord Croyton. "His idea is too new and untested and, therefore, objectionably risky. The initial capital expenditure won't supply a rapid enough return upon your investment. Profits will be virtually nonexistent for the immediate future and whatever *is* secured must be funnelled back into the mill for equipment renovation. But that," he ended with a thin-lipped smile, "is merely to name a few."

Mr. Bach's uneasy eyes narrowed until he regarded the earl through a pair of slits. He leaned back and interlocked his fingers upon his chest. "To name a few," he agreed curtly. "What may I do for you, my lord?"

"Would you declare the project completely unfeasible?" pursued Lord Croyton.

"No."

"Then your refusal stemmed from caution rather than any conviction as to its unworthiness?"

"Yes."

"And with sufficient incentive you might be persuaded to experience a change of opinion?"

"I might. You've studied Sir Antony's plans yourself?"

"Thoroughly," his lordship said dismissively. "I've had them from my man, Cal Jeffries, for about a week now. They appear sound, reasonable and surprisingly cautious," he judged, then admitted ruefully, "I, unfortunately, possess a more gambling nature, and my opinion is clouded by personal involvement."

"Your own man could advise you on the investment," Mr. Bach pointed out. "That is not why you're
here."

Lord Croyton stood and twirled his quizzing glass between thumb and forefinger. "No," he replied, "it is not.
I propose, sir, a trade."

"My support of Sir Antony," guessed Mr. Bach, and
he leaned forward and caught the other's keen gaze, "in
return for what?"

"A successful petition."

He lounged back again, slightly disappointed. "I've
been offered that before," he said unemotionally.

"Not by me," qualified his lordship. "Your petition
has been rejected four times over the past seven years. A
title is important to you, sir. I can secure it—easily."

Mr. Bach silently weighed his decades-old desire
against the cost.

"I'm not suggesting," interrupted Lord Croyton,
"that you bear the full brunt of Sir Antony's scheme. I
doubt that satisfying your titular aspirations could quite
recompense for such a risk. Therefore—strictly as an
agreement between ourselves, sir—I am willing to assume a twenty-eight percent share of the arrangement."

"Twenty-eight? That is an odd sum, sir."

"Not at all," the peer declaimed calmly and waved his
glass. "The figure merely represents the approximate
status of my current investments in your various enterprises. I prefer uniformity in my dealings, Mr. Bach. It
aids the memory. Have we an agreement?"

"Damme." The businessman swore beneath his breath
and examined his lordship momentarily before assent-
ing. "Twenty-eight percent, you say?"

The other nodded mutely.

"We have an agreement."

"Good," replied Lord Croyton and he returned to his chair. "Shall we commence discussion of the particulars?"

"You've an excellent grasp, my lord," Mr. Bach concluded scarcely an hour later. "I'll have my secretary prepare the necessary documents and I shall see your Sir Antony instantly."

"Please do. He's makin' a deuce of a nuisance of himself," lamented his lordship. Then he cautioned, "Be so kind as to remember, sir, that this is a *private* matter between ourselves."

"I shall remember," Mr. Bach assured him, and interrupted the earl's leisurely progress toward the door. "Forgive my curiosity, Lord Croyton, but why come to me? Why not simply supply your friend with the funds he requires?"

"He did not ask me," Lord Croyton answered. "And whatever his reasons or how I find them, I must respect his decision. Sir Antony is a friend and I value his friendship more than words can say. The fact that he chooses to confide his need to strangers rather than to me does not lessen its importance to me.

"In addition," he explained, "I adhere fastly to the axiom that one must never mix business with pleasure. A man such as yourself fulfills my three requirements. First, your interest and support of Sir Antony would not be considered unusual, thus allowing me to remain satisfactorily incognito and separate from proceedings.

"Second, you are vastly experienced, with a respectable reputation. Combined with Sir Antony's own quickmindedness and drive you will succeed where others would fail. My friend, Mr. Bach, will learn a great deal from you—to his benefit. And I have no doubt, sir, of the reverse."

He bowed and turned to leave.

"You said three requirements, my lord," prompted Mr. Bach.

"Minimal effort," supplied his lordship with a secret smile. "I knew not only which carrot to dangle but that I possessed the advantage in whatever bargain we struck. And believe me, I had other bargains to offer."

Mr. Bach returned the smile crookedly and queried: "You're *not* interested in business, my lord?"

"Not particularly," replied the earl, already vastly wearied of the discussion.

CHAPTER THIRTEEN

SET UPON A GRASSY PROMONTORY, Valstry presented an imposing facade to the world. A massive stone tower and a wall of Norman ancestry abutted the manor and stood as a stalwart reminder of the past. On each side of the grand house a small line of yews fanned outward. In the late earl's design, these trees served to envelop the curved drive and focus upon the Elizabethan edifice. He never saw completion of his plan and the present earl, whether through his own sense of aesthetics or sheer laziness, shelved his father's grandiose arrangements. The result was a charming mixture of the ordered and the chaotic.

This was never more evident than in the garden. Hidden behind the manor, its well-outlined paths led to secluded arbours enmeshed in masses of vines and branches. Huge elms offered comforting shade above conveniently located stone settees while roses, lilies and numerous varieties of forest flowers intermixed and bloomed in profusion. Colour was rampant and brilliantly alive.

The effect of this vision upon the casual visitor was often mixed. Most felt awed, others confused and still others amused.

Martin Costain was immensely pleased as he stood at the forest line just beyond the garden wall and watched Lady Elizabeth and Valerie Bach, who were seated on a stone bench in the garden. It had not taken long to dis-

cover the whereabouts of his missing heiress. He acknowledged that Valstry was the only logical place she
could be without alerting her family and the whole of
London society to the scandal.

Lord Croyton now seemed the primary obstacle to the
attainment of his financial happiness. It would have given
him immense satisfaction to have been called out that
night at White's and it was a monstrous wound to his
pride to have been thwarted by the preposterous dandy.

His luck at the gaming tables had swerved from fair to
disastrous; he was once again depleted of funds and
could no longer afford to wait patiently for the opportunity for revenge. It was time to give opportunity a slight
push and what better way than to snatch Miss Valerie
Bach from Valstry and involve George Bach and Reginald Croyton in a scandal for which they would pay
dearly.

Unaware of the observation, Lizzie glanced up from
her book and smiled brightly. "Look, Valerie, Mr. Wallace has discovered our hideaway."

"Oh! What...what a pleasant surprise," Valerie
gasped.

Mr. Wallace beamed appreciatively as he bowed over
her hand. "I found myself in the area on business," he
explained, "and thought to stop by. I do hope I'm not
intruding."

"No, no, of course not." She blushed and noted with
approval that he had lost considerable weight and his
clothes no longer strained with his every movement. He
would be amazingly presentable if only his face did not
still possess the tendency to redden at the slightest em-
barrassment. It was turning slightly pink now.

Lizzie directed him to a seat. "Do sit down, sir. I'm
certain we could all do with some refreshment," she said

suddenly. "I'll be just a moment, I promise. Excuse me, won't you?" With a blithe wave and a charming smile, she strolled off in the direction of the manor.

Lizzie was content to act the part of absentee hostess and pleased that Mr. Wallace proved able to visit. She had apprised him immediately of their plans and suggested a short stay as just the thing to turn Valerie's affections from Martin Costain.

So consumed was she with these thoughts that the news of yet another caller could evoke only the slightest interest. She entered the morning room listlessly and, without warning was seized in a crushing embrace and kissed.

"Lizzie! It's me!" Sir Antony laughed at her struggles and released her.

"I've the best news," he continued quickly. "I visited Brentshire and, damme, if I didn't find a way to make the place work for me instead of against me. I can make the mill run and in—oh, a couple years or so—I should even make a profit out of the thing.

"That's hardly the best of it, though. I've a partner and he's supplying enough capital to rebuild the place exactly to my specifications. I've already begun the work and I should, in fact, be there this moment." He grinned sheepishly and admitted, "But I thought to see you first."

"I'm very happy for you," replied Lizzie, dazed.

"Happy isn't the word for it!" exclaimed Sir Antony and continued to expound upon his newfound good fortune enthusiastically.

Lizzie retired to a settee and her eyes followed him as he paced the length of the room outlining the events of the past fortnight and his plans for the mill down to every board. She hardly took in his words, and knew that should anyone enquire of her what had been said, she would not be able to answer. Her feeble brain could not grasp the context of his speech and he spoke too quickly in terms wholly unfamiliar to her. The tiny room suffocated her.

"I still maintain controlling interest in the enterprise," he ended breathlessly after a quarter of an hour. "The land is mine and I have no intention of losing it. Do you know what this means?" he asked her finally and, without waiting for a response, announced, "We can be wed." At her silent stare, he added "Not immediately—there's a tremendous amount of work to be done but I should say by next year I shall feel confident enough to take on a wife. Lizzie?"

"I cannot think what to say," she admitted. "I am wondrous happy."

Sir Antony laughed as he sat beside her and cupped her hands in his. "You do not look it," he judged.

"It is only . . . must we wait still *another* year?"

"It is only a year and we will see each other."

"I don't wish to simply *see* you," complained Lizzie, quickly averting her gaze as the blood rushed to her cheeks.

Sir Antony gently rubbed her small, thin fingers in his and his heart quickened. "You cannot blame me for wishing things perfect for you. I need the year, Lizzie, and I feel certain Reggie will demand at least that long. He could not possibly agree to our union as affairs now stand."

"You haven't spoken to him, have you?" Lizzie did not need a verbal response, for he avoided her eyes. "Did you even see him?"

"Yes, I saw him."

"But you didn't broach the subject with him, as I asked—as you promised you would. Why didn't you ask him for help?"

"I don't need it," he replied stiffly.

"No, of course not, not now!" Lizzie retorted sharply. "But before! And even now..." She shook her head to regain coherent thought. "You never ask; you always state. *You* decide that we wait another year. *You* decide what is best and assume my compliance. I am not, however, so easily managed or so contrary as to suffer abrupt changes of heart by your command! Do you imagine yourself the only person with a modicum of pride?

"I wait and wait for an indication of your feelings and I finally receive it. I've listened to your plans for the future and I find no place for myself amongst them: yet, you assume my willingness to wait *another* year! You seem to think, sir, that you can walk in and out of my life whenever it serves you! You presume upon my affections too greatly, Sir Antony, just as you always have. You deliberately ignore my advice. You break your promises to me—"

Sir Antony intervened at her first break for breath. "I shall speak to Reggie the moment I return to London if it will make you happy."

"Oh, Tony," she murmured with a groan of immeasurable frustration, "must I be forever telling you what will make me happy?"

When Sir Antony mounted his horse a quarter of an hour later, he was decidedly aware that in some way, unbeknownst to him, he had failed. Admitting his fault and swearing more times than he could count that he would visit the earl could not ignite a sparkle in his beloved's eyes.

A movement in the wood caught his attention, and he cantered easily to the edge of the drive to investigate.

Out from the trees a black stallion emerged and galloped down the road. Sir Antony recognized the rider instantly. It was Martin Costain.

CHAPTER FOURTEEN

SIR ANTONY DISCOVERED upon his arrival in London that the plans for his estate demanded immediate attention. Innumerable visits with George Bach, meetings with various engineers and tradesmen, contracting for workers, learning and managing the accounts, as well as three visits to and from Brentshire served to fill his every waking moment.

He was not a man to waste time and energy, especially his own, and he dived into his task with a verve that was almost frightening. Never tiring, he moved from each new undertaking to the next with the agility and versatility of a chameleon. This mad drive towards accomplishment occupied his mind and drained his body so completely that each time he returned to London, he would recall his promise to visit Lord Croyton only to find some Herculean task requiring all his faculties intervening.

A week passed before he was seized by sudden resolution and found himself entering the Hanover Square library.

As he patiently—and somewhat anxiously, he conceded to himself—awaited the earl's descent from above stairs, he thumbed the litter upon the desk absentmindedly.

"Tony!" Lord Croyton greeted him from the open doorway. "You're late."

"Late?" asked Sir Antony, blinking.

"Thursday dinner. I was never more mortified when you didn't appear. Not a word from you. Had to drink that entire bottle of port. Well, that wasn't so intolerable, actually, but one should never be condemned to eat Cook's preparations alone. I shall overlook it because I'm well aware of how enmeshed you are with personal matters but I must tell you, dear fellow, that even *I* have never managed to forget an *entire* engagement. Although I can recall a few which I shouldn't have minded forgettin'."

"My apologies, sir," the baronet replied grandly, with a small bow.

"Tosh," retorted his lordship. "I cannot believe you're sorry to have missed that dinner."

"Then I am sorry to have missed the port."

"That—" the earl smiled widely "—I believe. What brings you today?"

Sir Antony accepted the indicated chair and watched with wry amusement as Lord Croyton nonchalantly perched himself upon the edge of his desk, swinging his leg back and forth.

"I promised Lizzie I would see you," he said and realized that he had begun the interview poorly, for the other raised an eyebrow. "What I meant to say is—"

A discreet knock heralded the arrival of Childers.

"Excellent idea, Childers," said Lord Croyton approvingly when he spied the servant's loaded tray. "Pour Sir Antony a glass of sherry, will you? I think he has need of it. None for me."

Fortified with liquor, Sir Antony began again. "I'm certain you're aware to some extent of how things fare with me," he said. "I've never made a secret of it. I was forced to sell the property in America simply to return to

England. I thought I should have to let Brentshire go to remain alive but I discovered something.'' Once embarked upon his plans, Sir Antony spoke tirelessly. His enthusiasm was tempered, however, by the abrupt realization of his dream's obligations brought by the past week and his companion's own thoughtful demeanour.

Observing Lord Croyton during his recital told the baronet little, for the earl's expression did not change from one of polite interest.

Sir Antony broke off in midsentence and ventured abruptly, ''What can I tell you that you don't already know?''

His friend blinked. ''Beg pardon?''

''I'm not a fool, Reggie. Although you could probably debate me on that point.''

''I'm hardly the one to debate you on any such point,'' Lord Croyton remarked dryly. ''And I do so hate to disillusion you, but I haven't the slightest idea what we're supposed to be talkin' about.''

''Renovation of Brentshire.''

''Ah, yes, well, I'm very happy for you.''

''Thank you.''

''Knew the tide would turn your way—bound to. Have everything you need, do you?''

''Without even asking.'' In spite of himself, Sir Antony smiled. ''Reggie,'' he commented quietly, ''did you think I wouldn't eventually reach the correct conclusion? I do trust you've enjoyed yourself but the jest is over.''

He stood and stated calmly, ''I can't accept it, Reggie.''

''Pity,'' commiserated the earl. ''Forgive me if I must ask what it is you can't accept?''

''The money.''

Sir Antony pulled a cheque received just that afternoon from his breast pocket and handed it to Lord
Croyton.

That estimable individual gave the paper an owlish
scrutiny through his quizzing glass.

"A cheque," he pronounced after satisfying himself of
the object's identity.

"Take it back, Reggie," pleaded Sir Antony.

"Back?" His lordship smiled sadly. "I should love to
take it, dear fellow, but I don't seem to recall that you
owed me anythin'."

"The first time I visited George Bach, he was not interested in my proposition," Sir Antony explained. "And
now suddenly he is. Not only interested, but almost
everything I could need or want is offered to me on a silver platter. All very neat and very precise and it didn't
make a damn bit of sense! I should have seen your hand
in that," he ended sarcastically.

Lord Croyton played with his quizzing glass and ignored the implied insult to his intelligence. "You signed
the contract with Bach," he stated simply.

Sir Antony laughed bitterly and waved the cheque at
him. "I wouldn't have this, otherwise."

"Then the money is yours."

His matter-of-fact tone caused Sir Antony to stop in
midstride. There was not a hint of emotion on the other
man's face.

"If I were you," his lordship continued without looking up, "I would take this money that poor besotted fool
gave you and buy some new clothes. I'm shocked you
haven't visited a tailor yet."

The baronet pressed him. "You're going to deny you
have anything to do with it?"

The earl sighed profoundly and grimaced. "My dear, dear friend, why are you so stubborn? If it will make you happy and less tiresome—then I confess." He raised his hands in mock surrender. "Guilty as charged. Now may we have an end to this inquisition?"

"What right did you have to interfere in my affairs? It was none of your concern."

"I beg to differ, sir." His lordship's voice lost its bantering tone and he faced his friend with an expression markedly resembling frosty antipathy. "My sister's happiness is very much my concern. Odd's fish, Tony," he pleaded, shaking off his distasteful demeanour in the process, "you don't seriously think I could let my future brother-in-law continue to make such a ass of himself? Since your return, that's all I've heard. Why didn't you come to me in the first place?"

He held up a hand as a pained look crossed his face. "Don't answer that! I'm quite certain I couldn't stomach hearing all your noble intentions. Sink me, you're not the only one who can be noble. And, if you hadn't acted so unreasonably meddlesome and atrociously inquisitive, I would have been so in peace."

Sir Antony smiled under this goodnatured harangue. "I am sorry, Reggie," he said. "But you also acted unreasonably meddlesome, I must point out. Very well, not 'unreasonably,' I grant you that, but you must try to understand my position. Don't you see the obligation you place me under? I could hardly come to you for money; how would that have looked? Besides," he ended lamely, "you had changed so."

A quizzical look settled on the peer's features. "It would appear that we've all changed, some more than others," he replied. "You've always been more than a friend—rather like a brother. And as far as debts are concerned, do you remember that time at school when I put—"

The baronet laughed. "I think that episode is best left forgotten," he advised.

His lordship continued his line of thought for a moment. "Yes. Well, at any rate, you got me out of it, for which I am eternally grateful. And that wasn't the only time, either. Now that the chance has come for me to return the favours, you have an ill-timed attack of nobility. Most tiresome."

"Perhaps you think so; perhaps I agree. But that doesn't alter the fact that you repay your debts in the most inconvenient manner."

"Forgive me," interrupted Lord Croyton, "but haven't we digressed from the purpose of your visit? Or was that charming preamble of your prospects merely given to entertain me?"

Sir Antony ignored the earl's comment and paced the room agitatedly. Except for the rhythmic tread of booted feet upon the carpet, silence soon settled over the two men. Lord Croyton, idly swinging his leg and quizzing glass in almost perfect synchronization, watched his friend sleepily.

"Lizzie—" Sir Antony broke the quiet with a mutter "—Gad, have I been such a fool? What do I do?"

Lord Croyton, startled out of his reverie, had surprising answers to both questions. "Yes, you have," he judged. "And what you can do first is stop that infernal pacin'. You're makin' me dizzy!"

Sir Antony stopped.

"The next thing you can do, and I repeat myself, is take that money and buy yourself somethin' decent to wear."

Sir Antony laughed and shook his head. His friend had an annoyingly persistent mind.

"Then," proceeded his lordship, "when you're properly attired, we shall both of us take a trip to Valstry, stopping along the way, of course, for the required nosegay—"

"No."

"No? Are you telling me now that you do not wish to marry my sister?"

"Reggie, you don't understand. Of course I want to marry Lizzie. I wanted to marry her the first day I saw her." Sir Antony's voice broke in frustration.

"Did you really?" Lord Croyton's mind searched back. The picture evoked of his sister as a child caused him to shudder. He sank into the nearest chair and waved a limp hand at his friend. "Then you're quite right, I don't understand. And the more I listen the less I understand. First you want to marry Lizzie, then you don't want to marry her, and now you do. Bless me if your pacin' isn't the only thing makin' me dizzy."

Sir Antony groaned as he retired into the chair opposite and enlightened his friend upon recent events. "She was just to be angry," he concluded. "I have ignored her feelings and taken advantage. I was wrong to approach her so."

"And not a single blossom in hand to demonstrate contriteness," added Lord Croyton. "Pathetic. I don't suppose you attempted to correct her harsh estimation of your character?"

"When everything she said was true? What could I say? If I had known then what I know now, I would never have visited Valstry."

"Finding oneself the recipient of one of Lizzie's tongue-lashings can be demoralizing," his lordship concurred.

"I meant in regard to you."

"Me?"

The room was darkening as the last of the sun's rays filtered through the window and Sir Antony shivered. Despairing of ever making his friend comprehend, he stared into the amber fluid in his glass and tried again.

"I love Lizzie with all my heart," he said, "and more than anything I want to make her my wife. I could not marry her if I had nothing to offer. Now that I have something, it's not yet truly mine. I have to make it mine."

In very terse words, he proceeded to describe the condition of his estate and enumerate the vast amount of work that would be required. He almost succeeded in convincing himself of the impossibility of his task. On his companion, however, the effect was minimal. Lord Croyton showed no sign that he was paying even the slightest attention. A sad smile worked at the corners of his mouth and he twirled his quizzing glass, seeming entirely absorbed by the play of light it produced.

"Do you see what I'm up against?" Sir Antony finished and wondered why he had bothered to explain.

Lord Croyton looked up and smiled triumphantly. "Actually, I do," he replied. "I must thank you, dear Tony, for explaining things so clearly."

He rose, walked over to the sherry, poured himself a glass and refilled Sir Antony's.

"If it had been anyone else, anyone other than you—" Sir Antony accepted the liquor "—it would be different. How can I accept your money when I could not take hers? It would be as if you were paying me to marry her.''

His own off-hand statement suddenly unsettled him and he searched the blank features across from him. ''Is there something about Lizzie you're not telling me?'' he asked.

''Is there something about Lizzie you don't already know?'' his lordship countered.

''Possibly. I have been gone for more than two years. We seem only to argue whenever we meet and the last time, she...'' A vision of Martin Costain reappeared before his eyes. ''Is it possible her feelings *have* undergone a change?''

Lord Croyton's eyes rolled upwards. ''Love! Does it make idiots of us all? Devil a bit, if it's not monstrous overrated.'' He took a delicate pinch of snuff while considering this insight.

Sir Antony accepted his response as a negative but asked sceptically, ''What about Costain—you can explain that?''

''Unfortunately—'' his lordship sneezed ''—I'm not at liberty to explain anything. You will have to take it on faith that it has nothing to do with Lizzie, or at least not in the way you're thinkin'.''

Sir Antony wished he could be more convinced when the snuff box lid closed with an abrupt snap.

''Clear your mind of all thoughts of Costain, or anyone else for that matter!''

The earl's staccato command caused Sir Antony to jump, but his voice returned immediately to its customary mellowness. ''As much as I hate to become involved, it would appear that between the two of you, you leave me no choice.'' He sounded much put upon and added, "I had envisaged a completely different role on this auspicious occasion—damme."

"What are you talking about?" Sir Antony demanded.

Lord Croyton looked disgusted, stood and began to pace himself. "I am of the opinion," he judged, "that at the moment the two of you should be monstrous ill-suited."

"What?"

"Ill-suited," enunciated his friend patiently. "You cannot decide if you want to marry her and she cannot decide if she will have you. If that isn't ill-suited, then—sink me!—I don't know what is. She says you haven't once considered her feelings—that you presume—and you don't argue with her? Damme! If that isn't a prime example of the pot callin' the kettle black, then I've never seen one! To make it worse, neither of you has given the least thought to my feelings on the matter—although that should hardly surprise me, considerin'."

Sir Antony sat in dumbfounded silence. "You're withdrawing your consent," he said slowly.

Lord Croyton frowned. "How can I possibly withdraw something which I haven't give in the first place? You can hold me responsible for your financial situation if you like," he stated. "But you seem to think that our business relationship precludes Lizzie's acceptance of your offer or that you can even make an offer. Utterly ridiculous! Lizzie knows less of business than I do; it just confuses the female mind. If she were ever to learn of our arrangement, it would certainly not be from me. And who else, besides yourself, is there to tell her?" He paused to allow this thought to sink in. "Besides, my agreement is not with you, dear fellow, but with George Bach. A trivial point, you may argue, but a point of fact nonetheless. As far as I'm concerned, if I wish to throw my money away that's my affair and no one else's." He paused again and added as an afterthought, "except perhaps my creditors."

He came to a halt before the desk and rapped a pile of papers sharply with his knuckles. "I do not consider that I've given anythin' away. You forget that I've known you for years. Despite superficial changes, you're still the same man. I fully expect an excellent return for my investment. In fact, I'll wager a thousand pounds you'll have full control in less than four years. So why you let your foolish nobility cloud your common sense is quite beyond me."

"That point aside, how you came by your change of fortune is one thing, how you use it is another. I cannot be responsible for that. At the same time, however, I cannot allow my sister to be carted off to—" he considered "—to paraphrase your own words, a musty worm-eaten pile of old sticks and bricks, now can I?"

Sir Antony was about to take umbrage when his pragmatic nature gained control.

"All of these objections, I could easily overlook," Lord Croyton concluded with a wave of his hand. "If I had the slightest evidence that you were compatible. But my patience has reached an end. I tell you—with the most heartfelt sincerity—that I have no desire to spend the duration of your marriage as an ambassador!"

"On that point, sir," Sir Antony replied, standing, "you need not be concerned. I was unaware of the depth of your feelings and I thank you for explaining them to me. I would like to see Lizzie when she returns from Valstry. With your permission, of course."

"Really, Tony, sit down."

"I understand your objections," the baronet continued, "for I expected no less, but I promised Lizzie only another year and that's a promise I do not intend to break."

His lordship turned, both eyebrows arched. "Another year?" he asked. "My dear fellow, pray tell how you escaped alive."

"Tosh!" Sir Antony borrowed the other's expression. "I don't believe you understand Lizzie as well as you think."

"Don't I?" He smiled and continued superiorly, "My sister is headstrong, tempermental and very much in love with you. For example, she has saved every one of your letters and reads them almost daily. No doubt she could quote them back to you from memory."

He paused briefly, turning to the window in disgust yet cleared his throat and began again softly. "Whenever you used to visit," he confessed, "Lizzie would scurry to the window to watch for you and then—" he smiled and waved his quizzing glass "—when she saw you, scurry away just as quickly for fear you might discover her there. Immensely silly behaviour, in my opinion."

"I can no longer read Lizzie's letters," admitted Sir Antony.

Lord Croyton turned back to his friend at his comment and observed, "Yet you keep them. Immensely silly behaviour, don't you think?"

"No. I am in love with her, Reggie," he answered firmly. "Don't doubt that."

"I don't."

Sir Antony smiled. "But you're not the one who needs to hear it, are you?"

In answer, Lord Croyton returned the grin broadly. "Stay to dinner? I do so hate to eat alone."

It was a moment before Sir Antony collected himself sufficiently to recognize the shift in topic. He would dine with the earl, but first, a matter required his immediate attention. He moved to the library door and hesitated. "Your wager's accepted, but I say full control in less than three years and every penny of your money back in less than five. It is good to see you, Reggie," he added and left before his lordship could respond.

Behind him, the only motion in the library was the gentle swaying of a silver quizzing glass between restless fingers. The gathering shadows gradually obscured the room, but Lord Croyton did not awaken from his preoccupied trance until Childers entered to light the wall sconces.

The faithful servant, believing himself unobserved, was startled at being suddenly addressed.

"Scurrying to windows? Saving letters?" the earl mused quietly. "What do you say to that kind of behaviour, Childers?"

"I do not know, sir," answered Childers when he regained his composure.

"I wonder," his lordship continued dreamily, but suddenly roused himself with a disgruntled snort. "Tosh! Love!" he remarked with distaste, "'tis a monstrous, overrated emotion entirely!

"Sir Antony will dine here tonight. Set two for dinner."

With those announcements given, Lord Croyton vacated the room abruptly, leaving his butler to question once again the sanity of the scion of this illustrious family.

CHAPTER FIFTEEN

LIZZIE OSCILLATED between abject misery at becoming angry and righteous indignation at Sir Antony's blithe and superior attitude. It served him well to be handed a setdown, considering all the torment he had caused in her life. Yet her temper—never manageable—had risen at what she could only describe as the worst possible moment. He had apologized, had promised to visit Reggie, she argued in calmer moments, yet a week passed without word of him.

She recognized her distress as fruitless and fought to control her chaotic emotions. She could not sleep and lost all desire for food.

Mr. Wallace called often and Valerie looked forward to seeing him so that Lizzie always felt obliged to discover some chore requiring her immediate attention. His visits, however, merely allowed more time for her own spinning thoughts, and as she tried desperately to occupy those moments with books and household tasks, she discovered with painful emptiness that the books held no interest and the household ran smoothly without her assistance.

She never shirked her chaperon duties, although she would have dearly loved to do so, and now watched her two friends from the parlour window. To observe them so obviously enjoying each other's company and laughing so carelessly did nothing to bolster her own sagging spirits.

She looked up often from her needlepoint and wondered at their conversation. As this line of mental endeavour only provoked recollections of her own happier garden encounters, she pushed the thought aside and returned to her work with a diligent and false fervour.

Valerie, she noticed after their short stay at Valstry, had become strangely distant and moody, unwilling or unable to confide in her. She smiled wanly at Lizzie's jokes, but Lizzie respected the underlying silence by keeping her own, and fretted at this sudden turn in her friend's spirits. Naturally, Valerie was distraught when they first arrived but Mr. Wallace's visits had cheered her. Now, when Lizzie had such high hopes for the two, the girl had reverted to her former mood. After three days of contending with Valerie's skittishness as well as her own, Lizzie's nerves jangled mercilessly at the smallest noise.

The announcement later that afternoon that Valerie had a slight headache was greeted, therefore, as if the complaint were fatal. Lizzie insisted she lie down immediately and arranged her pillows and ordered a cool compress.

She adjusted the compress slightly, smiling down at her friend. The girl's nerves were even more overwrought than her own, she decided, for Valerie had fallen asleep instantly.

As Lizzie retrieved the crisp muslin dress from the floor, a crackling of paper caught her attention. She removed the envelope and, about to place it on the dressing table, glimpsed something familiar in the handwriting. With a momentary qualm, she opened it.

She read the message twice before returning it, in its envelope, to the pocket. She placed the gown upon a chair and reached the top of the stairs before her knees buckled and she grabbed the banister for support as the room swayed about her dangerously. She felt alternately flushed and chilled. Her eyes refused to focus and her breath came in rapid gulps. *I'm about to faint,* she realized as she closed her eyes. *I never faint!*

This final thought evoked such a surge of anger that her lightheadedness disappeared instantly. *How dared they?* How could they use her so?! First Tony and now Valerie! What had she done to deserve all these lies? Was there no one she could trust?

For Valerie to deceive her twice, after all she had done, was unbearable! "Meet me tonight behind the castle parapet," the note read. It was signed by Martin Costain. It explained Valerie's mood change instantly. Did the silly girl think that she had saved her from Costain once, just to have the goose run back into his arms?! Reggie might have been correct before that it was none of her affair, but now was a different matter. Lizzie was not about to see Valstry used as a starting point in some sordid elopement.

The evening, as she knew it would be, was short. Valerie cried off from sitting with her friend, invoking The Headache, and retired early. Lizzie made no complaint and was all solicitousness for her ailing companion. She was, in fact, she explained, quite exhausted herself.

At half past eleven, she waited at the parlour window, and fifteen minutes passed before her suspicions were confirmed.

A dark-hooded figure stealthily emerged from around the corner of the manor. The unsuspecting girl moved furtively to the stand of trees which obscured the corner wall of the ancient fort.

Lizzie skirted the lawn towards the parapet seconds behind her friend. It was a chilly night and the moon flitted rapidly in and out from the clouds. She dodged behind bushes until the figure she sought was in view. Valerie had reached the small clearing at the far side of the garden.

Lizzie's heartbeat surged as she spied a figure step out of the forest. Valerie rushed to it and they clasped hands.

A large cloud overtook the moon's glow and blackness blanketed the scene as Lizzie dashed across the garden. She gasped as a sharp constriction about her waist drew her back abruptly and something was clamped down hard upon her nose and mouth. She panicked and fought against the obstruction until her lungs burst with the effort and the dizzy sensation from earlier returned violently. To avoid losing consciousness completely, she forced her body to go limp with a supreme effort of will. The hand over her nose moved and a rush of cool night air entered her starved lungs like a refreshing draught.

She panted for air as she was half-carried and half-dragged backwards into the higher bushes surrounding the garden. She could hear the rasping breath of her attacker. He tightened his grip about her waist and lifted.

She flew through the air and floundered in the darkness as, with a sudden lurch, the ground beneath seemed to shift. Her head cracked against the carriage door and she sank to the floor.

When Lizzie awoke, she had no clear idea of how long she had lain unconscious. Every muscle ached and a searing pain shot to her brain as she opened her eyes. Instinctively, she lay quiet and attempted to judge her position. The coach was travelling fast and a bump sent a wave of shock crashing up her spine. As the pain faded to an annoying thud against her temples, she opened her eyes again and discovered herself wedged on the floor beneath the seat. Although the position prevented unnecessary jostling, it cramped her legs painfully. She balanced herself carefully against the sway of the vehicle and rose to the seat.

She accustomed herself to this different rocking sensation and peeked out the coach window. The moon was behind a cloud; yet, riding to the side of the carriage, barely visible, was a lone horseman.

Memory returned to her in a rush. She was being kidnapped by Martin Costain! She shook her head to clear it and only caused her ears to ring. Costain wanted Valerie, not her. Costain didn't know he didn't have Valerie!

She remonstrated with herself to calm down and think rationally and then ranted at her stupidity for wearing her hood up and hiding her golden curls so beautifully. Costain possessed no means of knowing the identity of his captive and had not bothered to verify that he had snatched the correct woman.

There was only one solution. She would inform him instantly and he would take her back—or would he? One heiress was as good as another, and if he wanted revenge upon her or Reggie for the last episode, he could not have planned it better.

Any hope the thought of her brother evoked was followed quickly by despair. Reggie was in London and could not possibly know of her situation. No one knew or suspected. If Valerie deduced what had happened, would she tell? Who could she tell in time? Who was the figure she met by the trees, if not Costain?

Lizzie discarded these reflections as useless. She must help herself. She searched the coach desperately for a weapon.

Perched in the door scabbard was a riding pistol, and her hand rested on it in the dark. She drew it forth and felt tentatively along the barrel. She had never handled one before, for her brother detested weapons and she wondered if it were primed and loaded. On consideration of this new difficulty, she decided to postpone further investigation and not hold it more than gingerly until she was in better light.

Lizzie clutched the pistol between the folds of her cloak as the carriage came to a halt. There was a heated exchange between Costain and the jostlers as she surveyed the inn yard through the window.

The door opened abruptly, almost sending her spilling into the dirt, but a strong hand caught and dragged her from the coach. She studiously kept the hood well over her face as she was directed through the tavern doors and into a private salon.

"Stay here," Costain muttered into her ear.

Lizzie took quick measure of her surroundings the moment she was alone. She needed to discover an escape before Costain returned but, to be on the safe side, she checked the pistol first.

She possessed no definite knowledge, however, of what a primed pistol looked like and concluded for the sake of her morale that it was loaded. If it wasn't, then she would simply bluff Costain into thinking it was and compell him to take her back. She had little faith in her ability to do this, as her face was too expressive. She prayed that the gun would not fail her and that she would use it if she were forced to.

The salon, upon examination, was tiny but artfully designed. A small oaken table stood surrounded by chairs in one corner and two larger chairs sat before the hearth.

The fire crackled invitingly, but Lizzie ignored its proffered warmth and stalked about the room.

The most obvious escape route was a window directly
in front of her, but several attempts to open it proved
futile. She considered breaking the glass but, as this
would only bring someone running, decided against it.
Besides, the window gave directly into the yard, she noted
wryly. Someone was certain to remark her departure and
she abandoned that avenue with regret.

Exploration of the contents of the drawers in a tall bureau opposite the fire offered no help.

The only way out was the way in.

She had just turned back into the room in disgust when
the door opened and Costain entered. He threw his cloak
over a chair and spared her a sidelong glance before
moving to the fire.

"Looking for a way out?" he sneered.

Lizzie's heart thumped in her chest as she tried to keep
as much of her face in the shadows as possible.

"You're going to be disappointed, m'dear," he said.
"As you've no doubt discovered by now, the only way
out of here is through that door and the only way you're
going to get through that door is by leaving with me."

It struck her that he did not appear unduly surprised
at her silence and she wondered how long she could remain anonymous. He would expect Valerie to say something soon, as she did profess to love him.

Costain warmed his hands with his back to her. "This
time I will not be disappointed," he remarked over his
shoulder. "I'm confident you didn't tell Lady Elizabeth
about our little rendezvous. So no one will know you're
gone until the morning. By that time we'll be well away.
You disappoint me, though. I know you're silly, but I
never thought you would be so silly as to agree to meet

me alone. Especially after telling me you wanted nothing more to do with me. Pity, your little wish didn't come true, isn't it? I'm certain your father will agree with me.''

Lizzie smiled to herself despite her fear. Valerie was going to meet Costain to say goodbye. But the two figures in the garden she had been following—Valerie and who? Dexter Wallace! Valerie had confided her problem to Mr. Wallace and that gentleman had agreed to help. Of course he agreed to help; he was in love with the silly girl. Lizzie was forced to agree with Costain on that description; yet, at the same time, she admitted ruefully, she was not being too terribly clever herself. She should identify herself and demand to be taken back. She took a breath to do so and almost choked on it.

''It's also a pity I won't have the opportunity to meet Drenview,'' Costain was saying. ''I don't appreciate having my plans so rudely disrupted—especially by such an ass! The idiotic fool doesn't even know when he's been insulted and your 'dear sweet Lizzie' is a meddlesome bi—''

''How dare you speak to me like that!''

The words hung in the air.

Costain recovered first. His lip curled upwards slowly and his eyes twinkled dangerously. ''Well, this is an unexpected pleasure,'' he said and punctuated his silky words with a low bow. ''Lady Elizabeth.''

Lizzie's knees shook and her heart pumped furiously.

''Forgive my use of such ungentlemanly terms,'' he continued. ''I wasn't aware I was in such exalted company. Why don't you come closer to the fire? I'm sure you'll be more comfortable over here.''

''No, thank you,'' she whispered.

''You know, m'dear, I think this trip might actually become enjoyable.''

"You are going to take me right back to Valstry, sir," commanded Lizzie, summoning all the courage her strained nerves could muster.

"Am I?" he asked, and stopped his approach as her pistol rose.

"I have no desire to fire this thing, Mr. Costain, but I will if you do not take me back immediately."

After a moment's deliberation, the smile returned to Costain's face. "I don't think you will fire it," he predicted. "In any event, shall we—as your brother is fond of doing—consider the alternatives?

"I'll make my intentions clear to you and the decision will be yours. First, I do not intend to let you keep the pistol but neither do I intend to return you to Valstry, especially at gunpoint. You can give me the pistol now and we'll leave here peacefully or you can keep it and we won't.

"If you decide to keep it, I will try to take the pistol away from you. That gives you a second option. You can shoot or not. I much prefer you didn't, but that would make the pistol useless to you and we'd leave here as I planned."

He waved his hand. "On the other hand, if you shoot and hit me, at this range, it would probably kill me. I shouldn't particularly care for that—" he smiled at his feeble jest "—and if you've ever seen the inside of a prison, which I doubt, you wouldn't either. Now, if you miss, the gun would be useless to you again and we would leave here as I originally planned." He ended with a mocking sneer: "I am at your disposal, whatever your decision."

Lizzie swallowed with difficulty, and her eyes never strayed from Costain's throughout his list of alternatives. She believed he meant to retrieve the pistol; yet would he risk his life simply for revenge? He smirked at her condescendingly and his cold brown eyes betrayed nothing.

Time seemed to drag as her arms wearied and wavered and a sudden weakness pervaded her body. The smile on Costain's face broadened and he dashed forward as everything dissolved into a haze before her.

Lizzie shut her eyes and fired.

The blast sent her reeling backwards.

She heard Costain swear as he hit her arm and the pistol flew across the room and smashed against the bureau. He yanked her forward and crushed her against his chest, savagely ripping her hood from her head.

Lizzie opened her eyes to stare into the livid face of her captor.

"Wrong choice," he hissed down at her. "Luckily for us both, the damn thing wasn't loaded. Got it from my coach, didn't you? Well, I'll have to speak to my groom about his oversight. In the meantime, we're going to take a nice quiet ride to Gretna Green, and if you try anything like that again I'll break your bloody arm." His grip tightened painfully to underscore his words. "Do you understand?"

Not waiting for a response, he pushed her away and sent her spinning into the table.

Costain stooped to retrieve the pistol and answered the loud banging which had been going on at the door since the shot. He cursed beneath his breath and stepped quickly from the room.

Lizzie didn't hear what he said to the landlord, but when he returned he was smiling. "Pity your brother doesn't know where you are," he said. "I can think of nothing better than to be able to prick that inflated balloon." His eyes scanned her frame with malevolent de-

light. "Come to think of it, this might just be the way to
do it.

"Do move closer to the fire," he instructed as he noticed her tremble. "I wouldn't want you to catch a chill.
It will be a few minutes before they're finished changing
teams and we can continue our journey. But I don't suppose there's any rush, is there?"

Slowly, maintaining a safe distance, Lizzie moved to
the fire.

Costain, content to observe her through half-closed
lids, leaned back against the door and folded his arms
across his chest.

She sat down and her eyes scoured the room frantically but always returned to his arrogant expression.

He blocked the only exit. There was no help coming
and she had lost perhaps her only chance. She was
trapped, and even the loud noises and shouts from the
courtyard could not distract her attention from the hor-
ridness of her plight.

CHAPTER SIXTEEN

UPON LEAVING the earl's abode and calculating there being some little time to pass before the appointed dinner hour, Sir Antony strolled immediately to White's and was rewarded for his effort with the company of just the individual he sought, the inimitable Mr. Forbisher. Any other man's tolerance would have been tested to its endurance, but Sir Antony's placid good humour would not be shaken and he waited patiently for the discussion to turn to the topic which interested him most. He had been smiling for a full hour at his companion's boorish quips when his attention was suddenly aroused.

"...Dammed rude if you ask me," condemned Forbisher. "Not even a 'by your leave,' mind you. Ordinarily, I suppose one shouldn't expect even that much from Costain but really he was unbelievably brusque."

"Indeed?" Sir Antony prompted. "Was that about Martin Costain you were speaking?"

Mr. Forbisher eyed Sir Antony owlishly and sighed to himself over the younger generation. "I most certainly was! I mentioned that I was visiting him just last week."

"Yes?"

Sir Antony's interest mollified him and he settled into his seat with deliberation and warmed to his subject. "I would say it was about three of the clock. I had just stopped by for a...a chat," he said. What he had stopped by for was commiseration, for Count DeBoeulle's unex-

pected return from the North had promptly deprived Mr.
Forbisher of his customary afternoon company.

"I wasn't there more than a quarter of an hour, mind
you," he continued, "when of a sudden the fellow bun-
dles me out of there most rudely...most rudely, indeed.
Such manners!"

"Perhaps something of an urgent nature needed his
attendance?" Sir Antony suggested.

"Humph! What could Costain possibly have of an
urgent nature? Probably somebody dunning him, more
likely. That would explain his sudden departure."

"Departure?"

"Yes, heard him tell his servant that they would be
leaving for Kestelby?...Crastlebury?—some such place."

"Castleby?" Sir Antony supplied dully.

Forbisher smiled. "Yes, yes, that's the place. Dammed
odd name. Been gone about a week now."

"A week?"

"Yes, yes. Must I repeat everything I say? *I say!*"

Sir Antony leapt from his chair, moved quickly to the
door and in his haste, succeeded in knocking into one
poor gentleman attempting to enter.

Mr. Forbisher shook his head in dismay. The younger
generation was completely without manners. First Costain and now Russelford. All over some silly little town
no one had even heard of that had something to do with
castles. He nodded to himself, concluding again that it
was a demmed odd name for a town, and decided there
must be a castle somewhere about it.

Harvey Forbisher was partially correct. There once was
a castle near the small hamlet but that edifice had long
since disappeared and Castleby remained as a tiny vil-
lage of no more than a few tumbledown thatched-roof
cottages. One public tavern served as an inn for lost

travellers, for a person stumbling into Castleby was invariably lost. Its only point of historical noteworthiness was that the remnants of the castle which bequeathed the town its name could be found a mere quarter hour's carriage ride away—at Valstry.

Sir Antony sped through the streets of London and up the steps and through the door of Lord Croyton's town house. He caught Childers as he entered the hall and demanded, "Lord Croyton?"

The butler pointed up the stairs mutely and watched as the young baronet ascended three steps at a time. Once Sir Antony rounded the top, Childers sighed, spared one regretful glance up the stairs and closed the door to the street.

Bounding up to the landing left Sir Antony slightly out of breath, and he stopped for a moment to orient himself.

It was years since he had ventured this far into the house and he was thankful to find nothing changed. With a certainty of purpose, he opened the door which had once led to Lord Croyton's dressing room. It was still the earl's chamber, and occupied by the gentleman himself.

Lord Croyton glanced up from the contemplation of his visage in the dressing-table mirror and smiled at his unexpected visitor. "Tony!" he exclaimed. "Now you're early!"

With swift, florid movements he completed the intricate folds of his cravat. "Shame on you," he admonished. "You may be as late as you like, but never early. Bad manners."

He broke his concentration to watch his friend in the mirror. "Oh, dear, you're pacin' again. What have I done now?"

Sir Antony stopped behind him and glared. "You've refused to tell me about Costain."

Lord Croyton blinked at his reflection. "I do so hate to say this," he confessed with distress, "because you are my friend, but you are becomin' monstrous tedious. I repeat myself: I am not at liberty."

"Perhaps it would interest you to know, my lord," Sir Antony countered sarcastically, "that Costain has for the past week been in Castleby."

His lordship blinked again and returned to his tie. "Interestin' is hardly the word—amusin', perhaps? I wonder if Costain can be aware of the quality of entertainment to be found in Castleby. Come to think of it, is there *any* entertainment in Castleby?"

Sir Antony leaned one hand on the table and placed the other on the earl's shoulder. He bent to within inches of his friend's ear and spoke in a strong, clear voice.

"Reggie," he said, "there is something very wrong about this whole affair. I do not understand it, but I swear to you I will get to the bottom of it—with or without your help. Now, sir, the choice is yours. You can tell me what you know or come with me to Valstry."

"Really, Tony," replied Lord Croyton, swallowing, "too melodramatic."

Russelford's grip on his shoulder tightened. "God help me, Reggie, I love you like a brother but I am in no mood tonight for any foolishness. I'm worried for Lizzie's sake. Perhaps my worry is unjustified, but for my peace of mind I want it proven. As her brother, you have a duty to come with me. Now, you can do that on your own, or I can carry you out bodily."

"I never said I wouldn't go with you, dear boy," protested the other. "I think it an excellent idea, just as I did earlier. I do, however, have one question."

"Which is?" Surprised by the earl's acquiescence, Sir Antony released his grip.

Lord Croyton turned a blank stare into the mirror and, finding no help from that quarter, let out a long sigh. "I know," he murmured, "that I shall regret asking this." A pained expression crossed his face and he queried: "I don't suppose our trip could wait until *after* dinner?

"No? Why am I not surprised?" His lordship sighed again at Sir Antony's dark silence and he called to the valet, who had all the time been standing just outside the door, out of earshot of the baronet's threats. "Roberts, tell Childers to have the coach brought round."

"We ride," Sir Antony interrupted bluntly.

Lord Croyton raised a hand to waylay the servant. "Ride?" he asked.

"You know how long it takes by coach, Reggie. If we ride, we cut the time by half."

His lordship considered this argument. "Oh, very well. Two horses, Roberts, saddled and ready—and don't delay. *I* refuse to ride in these clothes."

Roberts returned in a flash and carried on his arm enough riding accoutrements for two. Within moments, he assisted the earl out of his fine evening raiment and into the more casual, comparatively plain sportsman's attire. He turned wordlessly to Sir Antony and moved to take the baronet's coat.

Sir Antony jumped from the valet's grasp. "Thank you, Roberts, I'm fine," he said.

"Don't be an idiot, Tony," commanded Lord Croyton, and he turned from reviewing his own tall frame to scrutinize that of his friend. "We are roughly the same size and Roberts is never wrong about a gentleman's attire. You can hardly expect to go riding in that—most unsuitable.'' He waved his servant on with a crisp "Roberts—"

Before Sir Antony could venture further remonstrations, it was too late. He resigned himself to the inevitable and was fitted into the earl's clothes swiftly and relatively painlessly.

He then discovered himself once more under the formidable scrutiny of the peer.

"Sink me," his lordship said approvingly, "if they don't fit you better than they do me."

This was not true. His lordship was always perfectly groomed; yet there was no denying some justification to the earl's remark. Lord Croyton was slightly thinner, so his clothes fit tighter on Sir Antony, which accentuated the length and strong musculature of that gentleman's legs. The straight lines made him appear taller and his broad shoulders massive.

Sir Antony shrugged off the compliment. "Shall we go?" he urged.

Lord Croyton bowed him through the door gracefully and out to the two mounts awaiting them in the street.

SIR ANTONY LED THE WAY and, once free of the twisting city avenues, set a gruelling pace across the countryside. He had no doubts of Lord Croyton's ability to ride hard and, except for the occasional listen to the reassuring pound of hooves behind him, gave all his thoughts over to what lay ahead.

It was just past midnight when at an unslackened pace, he rode onto the Valstry grounds and, jumping from his horse, mounted the steps to the mansion in a trice. It was Lord Croyton, therefore, following at a much slower pace, who first noticed the dark figures standing still in the lawn.

"Ho, there!" he called pleasantly and ventured closer when the shadows did not move. "Miss Bach, is that you?" He asked.

"Oh!" was the terrified response.

Sir Antony tramped impatiently down the steps to see what delayed his friend.

"What the devil's going on here?" he demanded upon spying the man and woman cowering in the moonlight. "Who are you people and what are you doing?"

Mr. Wallace stepped forward. "Lord Croyton? I apologize for meeting you like this. My name is Dexter Wallace."

Sir Antony accepted the proffered hand before he realized the gentleman's mistake. "I'm not...this is Lord Croyton," he muttered, nodding towards his lordship.

"Oh!" Mr. Wallace snatched back his hand, embarrassed. "I'm terribly sorry, I thought...well, the way you came over...what you said—"

"Quite all right, Mr. Wallace," interrupted Lord Croyton. "My sister has told me about you. Pleasure to meet you at last."

"Yes, well, er, I could wish for better circumstances."

Lord Croyton looked at Valerie sympathetically. "Of course—" he coughed "—I can't help thinkin' it might be somewhat better if we moved inside."

Sir Antony's impatience grew to intolerable proportions as the servants were roused, the household settled and the couple calmed before an explanation of their night walking could be delivered.

In the parlour's light, Valerie peered at the angry and stern stranger with Lord Croyton.

"What's goin' on here?" he demanded.

She quailed beneath his flashing blue eyes and, shrinking back into her seat, answered meekly, "Going on?"

"Yes," he insisted, "goin' on! Where is Lizzie and what were you two doing in the garden?"

Tears rose to her eyes and her hands waved uselessly. Mr. Wallace gallantly came to her rescue with a linen and a comforting arm.

"Odd's fish, dear boy, you do have a persistent mind," protested his lordship as he studiously ignored the tender scene before him. "I warn you that Miss Bach happens to be the daughter of your generous partner. I should be more careful if I were you in how you choose to address her."

"You're George Bach's daughter?"

Valerie nodded with a sniff.

"Demme!"

"Really, Tony."

"Why didn't you tell me sooner?"

"You didn't let me."

"My apologies, Miss Bach, but I must know where Lizzie is."

"In bed?" Valerie suggested.

"You expect me to believe that she retired so early?" he countered.

"Why not?" Mr. Wallace blurted out.

"Yes, why not?" his lordship chimed in. "In the country, one goes to bed frightfully early. Nothing else to do."

"Yes, yes," Valerie blubbered. "Lizzie said she was going to bed at the same time I did."

"See?"

"And with all this noise, she hasn't woken up?" Sir Antony persisted.

"Point," Lord Croyton admitted, and he summoned a servant and requested that his sister be wakened immediately to join them.

"Now, then—" he turned to the couple staring at him from the settee "—I do think an explanation is in order. Was there a reason for your roamin' about the grounds after midnight?"

Valerie sniffed and Mr. Wallace coughed.

"Answer His Lordship," Sir Antony reprimanded sternly.

Mr. Wallace straightened his shoulders and frostily directed his comments to the baronet. "I will be quite happy to answer his lordship, sir, since this is his house and Miss Bach is his guest. He has helped her in the past and he has every right to know. But I do not know who you are, sir, and I do not blithely tell tales to strangers, or obey commands so rudely given. I refuse to say another word in your presence," he concluded, and returned his attentions to Valerie in cool defiance.

Lord Croyton stayed the angry rebuttal from his friend. "He does have a point."

"Dash it! Very well, I'll wait outside."

His stormy departure was interrupted by the entrance of an extremely unhappy servant.

"Her ladyship is not in her chamber," the butler said with reluctance. He cleared his throat in the silence that followed this declaration and then announced, "The house has been searched but she is nowhere to be found. I'm having the grounds searched now." He bowed and quickly withdrew.

Sir Antony stopped in his tracks. He had never truly imagined it was possible for anything to happen to Lizzie and had convinced himself that he would once again come away looking the fool. He was angry, more at himself for allowing it, than for any other reason.

He stared into Lord Croyton's clear blue eyes and realized that between his own anguish and Reggie's foolish banter, he hadn't considered that the earl might actually have been worried.

The spell was broken as Valerie burst into tears. The earl blinked and the corner of his lip curled upwards into a sad smile.

He spoke to Mr. Wallace in a voice the baronet had never heard in all the years of their acquaintance. It was soft, controlled, yet undeniably commanding.

"Mr. Wallace," he said, "this gentleman is Sir Antony Russelford, a very dear friend. What you can say to me can be said to him, as well. It will go no further than this room, I assure you. Now, sir, kindly tell us where my sister is."

"I don't know, sir," gulped Mr. Wallace.

Valerie struggled through her tears and regarded the baronet with awe. "You're Tony?" she asked. "Lizzie's mentioned you. But I didn't know that's who you were."

Sir Antony smiled down at the teary-eyed girl. "Yes, I'm Tony. Where is Lizzie, Miss Bach?"

"I don't know definitely, but if it's what I think then it's ... it's absolutely dreadful! Poor Lizzie! And it's all my fault! Oh, all my fault!"

"What's dreadful, Miss Bach? Please tell me. Does it concern Martin Costain?"

Valerie rewarded Sir Antony's patient questioning with renewed sobs.

"You know?" Mr. Wallace broke in, confused.

"You seem to," Lord Croyton pointed out.

"Miss Bach told me," the gentleman countered.

"I don't know anything!" Sir Antony admitted as his frustration mounted again. "All I want to know is where the devil Lizzie is!"

"I think Martin..." whispered Valerie. "I heard something when we were in the garden. I couldn't be certain, of course, but... but it sounded like a... a carriage. I don't know how...or...oh! She must have read the note!" wailed Valerie.

Lord Croyton and Sir Antony exchanged bewildered glances.

"Note?"

"Oh, my God," breathed Mr. Wallace. "Certainly not."

"Oh...oh," the girl shook her head hopelessly. "I know she did. She must have."

"What note?"

Mr. Wallace grimaced slightly but replied honestly, "For the past week, Miss Bach has received numerous messages from this man Costain. I believed that agreeing to see him as he wished would put an end to the harrassment. She was to meet him at midnight behind the parapet in the garden. He never appeared."

Valerie found her voice with a croak. "It was me he wanted! Surely he won't take her all the way to Gretna Green. He'll bring her back when he realizes his mistake."

"I doubt that," Lord Croyton said with a certainty that caused Sir Antony to look sharply at his friend.

His interrogation was interrupted by the announcement that Lady Elizabeth was definitely not in the house or on the grounds.

"Have a coach brought round immediately," Sir Antony ordered.

The servant responded instantly to the voice of authority and the baronet paced with long purposeful strides across the room. He glanced up to find the earl regarding him with one cocked eyebrow.

"The horses won't do?" Lord Croyton asked.

"The horses are too tired and when we find Lizzie, we'll need the coach," he replied shortly. "From the sound of it, he hasn't too great a lead on us, but I wish I could be convinced that he'll head north again."

His lordship gave him a thin-lipped smile and his old manner returned completely. "We are all of us creatures of habit, m'dear Tony," he pronounced. "Costain's no different. Besides, it's closer."

"I realize, Lord Croyton," interrupted Mr. Wallace, "that it is not my place, but I am grateful for the kindness you have shown Miss Bach. You see—"

The earl held up his hand quickly. "Please," he begged, "don't tell me you're in love or I shall be most decidedly ill."

"I am in love, sir."

"I don't know why I bother," lamented his lordship. "Nobody listens to me."

"I am aware of the risk you took the first time," Mr. Wallace continued, undaunted, "for a woman you didn't even know. You saved Miss Bach from Martin Costain. Now, it's *your* sister and I feel partially responsible. If I hadn't told Miss Bach to meet Costain, none of this would have happened. I should like to help in any way I can."

"Thank you," Lord Croyton responded after some thought and nodded towards the lady leaning so contentedly against the other man's shoulder. "But I do think that you'll rather have your hands full here."

"Is this what all the bad blood was about between you and Costain?" Sir Antony demanded. "Did you challenge Costain over Miss Bach, Reggie?"

Both of the earl's eyebrows shot skyward. "What is this penchant my family and friends seem to have for wanting to see me murdered?" he cried. "I didn't challenge anyone over anythin'—but that doesn't mean he got what he wanted. So may we close that particular chapter in my past?"

Sir Antony laughed at his friend's request. "I never knew you had it in you!" he declared.

Before his lordship could devise an appropriate retort, their carriage arrived.

"Mr. Wallace?" Sir Antony broke into the couple's low conversation. "Lord Croyton and I are leaving now. I must ask you to do the same."

Mr. Wallace nodded his understanding. "I'm leaving now also," he said, bowing gracefully to the girl, "with the express understanding that I shall return tomorrow."

Valeries' eyes lowered and a faint blush rose to her cheeks.

The other two gentlemen ignored their tender parting as much as possible, but the moment they settled into their coach his lordship broached the subject.

"Now that is a couple suited for each other," he pronounced.

"Um?"

"Mr. Wallace and Miss Bach—definitely suited," explained Lord Croyton. "Blissfully ignorant of everythin' goin' on around them. How can one allow oneself to get into such a state?"

Sir Antony tactfully ignored the obvious answer and changed the subject. "Reggie, I believe I owe you an apology," he said.

"Do you?"

"Yes. I should have believed you about Costain. Should have known it had nothing to do with Lizzie. I've been rather upset lately."

"Have you? Hadn't noticed. Apology accepted, at any rate. Now I believe *I* owe you one."

"For what?"

"*I*—" the earl stressed the pronoun "—should have believed *you* about Costain. How did you know he'd gone to Castleby?"

"I saw him there when I visited Lizzie, but I didn't know he'd been there this entire week until I spoke to Forbisher."

"Harvey Forbisher?"

"The same."

"Sink me." His lordship lounged back to digest this bit of news and, after long deliberation, concluded wryly: "That's the last time I criticize his waistcoat."

Sir Antony made no reply to this cryptic statement.

Silence prevailed in the coach as the miles sped by, and Sir Antony peered constantly through the window as if expecting to come upon their prey at any moment. All he saw were dark clouds threatening from the north.

As Spaulding drove the horses onward through the night, the baronet fervently hoped that they would be able to outrun the worst of the storm.

Suddenly, a break in the clouds startled him. The moonlight hit the road before him with brilliant clarity and illuminated a dark, hooded rider perched in the middle of the gravel path.

CHAPTER SEVENTEEN

SPAULDING CRACKED THE WHIP loudly above the horses and drove down upon the vision. He would not be stopped by another highwayman, and the coach bolted forward, thundering toward imminent disaster.

The horseman froze.

An instant before the lumbering carriage struck, his horse reared frantically to escape and sent its rider twirling high into the air.

Barely audible above the crush of wheels, a pistol resounded.

The passengers were tossed about violently as they careened to a halt.

Sir Antony jumped to the ground and took quick stock of the situation. He leapt up into the box beside Spaulding and discovered the reins dangling between the driver's useless fingers. The shot had merely grazed an arm but the wound bled profusely through the man's coat. Turning him toward the lamps, Sir Antony examined the arm and the ashen, stricken face carefully.

"Nothing serious, Spaulding." He smiled reassuringly. "The bleeding should stop in no time. Let's get you down."

Lord Croyton joined him and they settled the coachman against a wheel. So involved were the two gentlemen in their driver's misfortune that they failed to notice

the horseman. Recovered from his fall and deserted by
his mount, he approached the small party cautiously.

Sir Antony knelt beside the wounded man and
searched for something to tie off the injury. In desperation, he began to undo his cravat.

"Not your tie!" Lord Croyton objected.

"We haven't anything else," he responded sensibly.
"Unless you'd like to volunteer yours."

"No, no," replied the earl quickly. "I trust your
judgement."

With a laugh and a shake of his head, Sir Antony
resumed his ministrations.

Spaulding was the first to notice the approaching gun-
man and his mouth worked frantically. Finally, realizing
his inability to communicate in such a fashion, he gestured wildly towards the man.

A firm hand on Sir Antony's shoulder interrupted his
rise.

"Trust my judgement in this," his lordship said. "See
to Spaulding, will you, dear fellow?" he asked and,
walking a few steps forward, stopped and waited for the
other.

"Now see here, you!" Lord Croyton began testily.
"My patience has worn thin! You're a damnable nuisance and it's high time I did something about you. I
cannot abide this continual inconvenience. Not only have
you broken your promise—which is unforgivable in itself—but you must needs go and shoot my driver."

The man tried to speak but his lordship continued un-
abated.

"Twice is understandable—coincidences do happen—but three times quite strains credulity," he complained. "Now, I'm a reasonable man and it is possible,

since you do work at night, that you failed to notice when last we met the insignia on the coach. You will not forget it in the future, I guarantee. I will have you off the road, sir, and no longer harrying weary travellers—particularly me! Do you understand?''

Any hesitation Sir Antony felt at permitting his friend to handle the situation vanished instantly, and his amazement grew by leaps and bounds as the highwayman hung his head like an errant schoolboy.

''Aye, sir,'' he replied meekly.

''Good.'' Lord Croyton nodded his satisfaction at the conclusion of the interview.

The robber cleared his throat apologetically. ''Beggin' yer pardon, milord,'' he ventured, ''I dinna mean to shoot yer driver but he wouldna stop. As it was—I only nicked 'im and 'im almost runnin' me down like 'e did.''

''Then you should consider yourself exceedingly lucky on both counts,'' quipped his lordship disdainfully. ''If you had done any more damage, I should have to shoot you myself and I abhor the sight of blood. Now get out of here before I overcome my distaste.''

He rejoined Sir Antony by the coach and motioned towards Spaulding. ''How is he?'' he asked.

His task neglected, Sir Antony quickly bandaged the arm and looked up guiltily. ''He'll be fine, but we should get him to a doctor,'' he replied. ''Of course, he won't be able to hold the horses with that arm, so one of us will have to drive.''

''Damme, I've no objection to driving, mind you, but trying to find a doctor at this hour—'' the earl complained petulantly. ''I'm afraid it will put them monstrous far ahead.''

''Not likely, sir.''

Instead of making good his escape as advised, the highwayman defied common sense and drew closer.

"You're still here?" his lordship asked indignantly.

"'Cuse the interrupt, gennum, but I know these roads like the palm o' me 'and. And I know me 'orses—I rec'nized those greys when they passed an' I figured yer lordship might be followin'. That's why I stopped ye," he ended, immeasurably pleased with himself and his logical deduction.

"So far you have not endeared me to your cause," said Lord Croyton with a frown. "I do trust there is more to your tale."

"There is. I didna stop ye to rob ye—I ne'er go back on me word. Like I said, when I seen those greys I remembered 'em. Ain't likely to ferget such fine beasts an' all. I follered 'em. Thinkin' as how if ye was to come along, milord, ye might want to know where they went." His dark eyes gleamed in the coachlight.

"Where did they go?" demanded Sir Antony.

"They turned off the main road about 'alf a mile a'ead turnin' into the Gracious Arms. That weren't more'n ten minutes ago," he said and added speculatively, "They got themselves a doctor at Burnington jus' north o' there."

"Reggie! Help me get Spaulding into the coach. I'll drive."

"Beggin' yer pardon, sir," the bandit interrupted again with a woeful shake of his head, "but that road ain't in the best o'repair, if ye be gettin' me meanin'. 'Specially what wi' the rains they been 'avin' in these parts o' late." He made a skyward gesture at the menacing clouds to illustrate his point. "Gonna rain again most likely any minute," he predicted. "If ye ain't careful or don' ken the road, ye could end up in worse shape than yer driver there. Seems to me, sir, and I ain't pryin', mind ye, but ye both got a bit on yer minds. Ye got to be payin' attention on that road.''

"It don't signify," cried Sir Antony. "We haven't a choice."

Lord Croyton regarded their new found ally oddly. "Do you *ken* the road?" he asked softly.

The man's eyes crinkled above his mask. He puffed his chest out proudly and announced, "Like I said, milord, like the palm o' me 'and.''

Encumbered though he was with Spaulding, Sir Antony foresaw his lordship's intention immediately. He extricated one hand from his task and grabbed the earl's arm. "Reggie, are you daft?"

His friend ignored the question. "Then you shall drive us," he said to the highwayman. "First, though, do remove that silly mask. We can hardly go about scaring everyone in Burnington—or wherever it is we're going."

The small man struggled with his mask. "Lord!" he exclaimed in his excitement. "I'd be right 'onoured to ride up behind those beasts. I would indeed!"

"Then be quick about it. We're in a hurry."

Unceremoniously bundled into the coach, Sir Antony protested the decision vehemently. "That was not a good idea, Reggie," he stated. "Letting a confessed thief drive us. Have you lost your senses?"

Lord Croyton was all practicality in the face of his friend's distress. "The man does seem to know his horses," he responded. "I've always had a suspicion about Costain's greys."

The coach started immediately and he nodded his approval at the pace. "I suppose I could drive but I'd more than likely put us in some ditch somewhere," he added.

"And you could drive but that would leave me here to tend Spaulding. You know how I feel about blood. All in all, I think the solution quite equitable."

"I'm almost afraid to ask," Sir Antony began, "But you do seem acquainted with the fellow. How—"

"Don't ask!" the earl burst out testily. "I absolutely refuse to attempt that again!"

Realizing that his friend could not possibly understand the allusion, he promised in a far calmer manner, "Someday, when I can be guaranteed there's nothin' else on your mind, I may tell you the story.

"We shall have you to a doctor as soon as possible, Spaulding."

"Thank you, milord," came the quiet response.

"How are you holding up?"

"With all due respect, sir," the coachman sighed deeply, "I'm not a young man to be handlin' all this excitement." He paused significantly and announced what had obviously been a difficult decision. "I've a daughter what lives in Kent—a quiet life, milord, that's for me."

Sir Antony watched his friend's face distort into a vivid picture of dismay in the dim light.

"I quite understand, Spaulding," his lordship commiserated regretfully. "Recently, life has been rather... hectic?"

"Yes, sir," agreed Spaulding with feeling.

Lord Croyton rested back and tapped his quizzing glass against his lower lip. "But that does put me in a bit of predicament," he murmured. "What do I do for a coachman?"

The carriage swerved from the main road and the ride grew bumpier as they hurtled down the side avenue to the Gracious Arms. It was a sharp, dangerous turn at the gruelling pace at which they were travelling; yet the passengers experienced no discomfort.

Sir Antony could distinguish little in the darkness, but as the glint of light off the earl's quizzing glass was fixed motionless for a second, only to disappear, he became alarmed. He barely perceived the outline of his friend's head in the gloom as it turned towards the partition separating passenger from driver.

"You are daft, Reggie!" he breathed.

His lordship's tranquil voice drifted to him from out of the shadows. "The perfect solution, old chap. Must get the fellow off the highways; he's become a deuce of a pest to me. I suppose I could put up with that ordinarily, if he wasn't such an expensive one. If my life continues in this manner—heaven forbid!—it would be cheaper for me in the long run to have him where I can see him. Vastly cheaper."

There ensued a long pause.

"Besides," he said eventually, "He *is* an original. And I'm always curious to try new things. One mustn't get into a rut, y'know."

This prosaic, matter-of-fact announcement was greeted by an explosion of laughter from Sir Antony.

"Forgive me," the soft voice asked blandly, "but did I say somethin' amusin'?"

"It is my considered opinion, Reggie," Sir Antony assured him, "that you will never get into a rut."

"Well, I do hope not. I shouldn't have the faintest idea of how to get out again."

Sir Antony let that comment pass unanswered. He was smiling from pure enjoyment for the first time in days when the coach lurched over a stone and brought him abruptly back to reality.

CHAPTER EIGHTEEN

THE EARL'S COACH pulled into the Gracious Arms, and Sir Antony hopped out before the carriage had completely stopped.

Costain's equipage sat in full view and he chafed impatiently at his lordship's more sedate descent. He pulled the earl aside.

"Reggie, I know it isn't my place and I don't mean to usurp you in this or insult your courage, but—damn it all!" He floundered miserably, trying to phrase his request.

Lord Croyton blinked as the corner of his mouth turned up slightly. "No offense taken, dear boy," he said. "I have always maintained a particular distaste for the sight of blood. I've never denied it, and these situations are often—" he groped for the word "—rather distasteful. Now, don't you think you'd best get in there?"

Sir Antony disappeared before the earl finished speaking.

"Besides, I rather think Lizzie would prefer it," he remarked.

He turned back to the coach and finally got a full look at the man standing, hat in hand, beside the carriage. With mask removed, the highwayman resembled ever more the loyal canine, as bewhiskered, drooping jowls tugged at his eyes and brought them downward in a forlorn questioning expression. A curly mop of hair met his bushy eyebrows and concealed his forehead. He stood considerably shorter than the peer and bounced nervously from foot to foot under his steady gaze.

"You say this place has a doctor?" his lordship asked.

"Burnington does—yes, milord."

"Then take me to him, please," instructed Lord Croyton and he moved to climb into the coach.

The highwayman cleared his throat. "Beggin' yer lordship's pardon, sir," he mumbled, "ah . . . well, I was jus' wonderin' . . . I mean seein' as 'ow . . ."

"We must do something about that stammer, and those clothes will definitely not do." The earl frowned and he added with a sigh, "But I suppose we simply haven't the time now. I would like to get Spaulding to this doctor before he bleeds too terribly all over my coach, if you don't mind."

More throat-clearing stopped him again.

"If you have something in your throat, man, do get it out," he demanded.

"What are you goin' to do with me?"

"Do? Well, if you can manage to get back up into that driver's box and take us to the doctor, I might consider takin' you on as head groom. You have a fine knowledge of horses and an excellent hand on the reins."

The highwayman's jaw gaped in astonishment.

"If you don't," he continued matter-of-factly, "I shall have you boiled in oil and strung up by your heels." This thought provoked a small smile. "Wonderfully appealin' idea," he judged.

The man's mouth snapped shut.

Lord Croyton brushed a speck of dust from his sleeve and seemed to realize that the other had not answered. "Well?" he prompted.

The highwayman cocked his head and examined his prospective employer keenly. There was nothing in the bored eyes, the bland expression nor the dandy's stance to indicate anything other than acute indifference. Before he could respond, however, the earl spoke again.

"If you accept, there are three tenets you would do well to remember as my employee," he began crisply. "I do not abide dishonesty—in anyone. I will not tolerate disobedience among my employees. And I abhor laziness, but I do enjoy a peaceful life, or—" he considered the inn sadly "—I did. If you can remember these, we shall get along splendidly."

The footpad met the pair of cool eyes directly and did not mistake their message. The posing beau had confused him; yet now there was not a hint of indifference or indecision in the stance or gaze of the peer.

A sly grin spread across his grizzled features and he started for the box, saying: "Aye, sir. The doctor, sir."

"Oh, by the by," his lordship drawled, "what is your name?"

"Evan, milord. Jus' Evan."

"Well, 'just Evan,' my name is Croyton... Reginald Croyton. See that you don't forget it."

Evan nodded.

"Shall we be off then?" said the earl with a smile.

SIR ANTONY HAD LEFT Lord Croyton with mixed feelings. When he entered the inn, however, he felt only rage, and his entrance generated sufficient noise to alert his quarry. Hearing the commotion in the common room,

Costain positioned himself with a commanding view of the door.

"It would appear, m'dear—" he addressed his captive "—that I'm not to be completely disappointed. I must re-evaluate your brother's perceptiveness. Perhaps he's not such an ass after all."

The superior smirk which covered his face froze on his lips as the parlour door was flung open. The intruder was not Lord Croyton.

Lizzie flung herself from the chair and raced across the room into the baronet's arms with enough force to send a lesser man reeling.

"Tony! Oh, Tony! I'm so glad—" She cried freely, and buried her face in his shoulder.

Sir Antony wrapped a protective arm around the weeping girl and lifted her gently out of the doorway. He kicked the door shut behind him. There was no pleasure in his voice when he spoke.

"It's all right, Lizzie. I'm here now. Did he hurt you?"

Lizzie gulped back her tears and shook her head against him. "No," she choked out.

"It's very fortunate you didn't, sir," he directed sternly at Costain.

"And what business is it of yours?" Costain sneered. "I don't even know who you are."

"People tell me I've changed, so I'll believe you don't remember me. Allow me to reintroduce myself—" he bowed shortly "—I'm Antony Russelford."

"Pleasure to renew our acquaintance, Sir Antony. I do recognize the name, and you *have* changed." Costain returned the bow and with the pleasantries attended to, his smile disappeared. "I also recognize that I've seen you about a few times and I begin to think you almost as meddlesome as her ladyship. Now, what concern is this of yours?"

"Lady Elizabeth is betrothed to me, sir."

This announcement provoked not only a surprised look from Costain but a gasp from Lizzie.

She repositioned herself slightly to gaze at the granite face above her. His lips formed a thin line and his square jaw was locked tight. Sir Antony spared not a glance at her, but stared at Costain unblinkingly. Even the angriest most stubborn she had seen him could not compare to this. At that moment, she did not give much for Costain's chances—or her own.

The object of Sir Antony's wrath, however, was feeling anything but intimidated. "I wasn't aware Lady Elizabeth was engaged—" he smiled and motioned breezily at Lizzie "—and it would appear neither was the lady."

"Circumstances have prevented the usual announcement. You will excuse us."

Annoyance at being thwarted for a second time registered in Costain's voice. "I don't believe I will. You think, Sir Antony, to barge into a private salon and give orders. I'm not so easily commanded."

"We can settle this another way, if you prefer."

"I do," insisted Costain with a smirk.

Lizzie's heartbeat skittered wildly. This was madness! The next question and answer stopped her cold.

"Do you have a preference of weapons, sir?" Costain asked coolly.

"Swords."

"I shall see what there is available."

Sir Antony moved aside to allow the other to pass and propelled Lizzie to the hearth.

She regained her voice. "You can't duel him, Tony."

"Kindly refrain from telling me what I can and cannot do," the baronet replied bluntly.

"Tony!" Lizzie gasped looking up into a pair of very cold blue eyes. The anger she saw caused her to push back against him but she was locked in an iron grip and could only search his face desperately for some hint of his thoughts.

The one possible explanation was that he believed her capable of going willingly with Costain. Surely he couldn't believe that. But how had he discovered her missing? Had he come alone? So many questions whirled in her brain and found expression in one word.

"Tony?" Her voice cracked.

"We'll talk later" was the harsh response.

Costain returned before she could think of a reply. Sir Antony grasped her arm and guided her towards the door.

"Wait outside," he said.

Lizzie stared in morbid fascination at the two swords Costain nonchalantly placed upon the table.

He removed his coat and cast a disparaging glance at the rough-hewn floor, shaking his head. With a swish of his right arm, he weighed the blades in turn and nodded his satisfaction after each test.

"No! I'm not leaving."

Instead of arguing, Sir Antony dropped her arm. "As you wish, but stay out of the way," he instructed.

He removed his greatcoat and spencer and placed them carefully on a chair. Once stripped to shirtsleeves, he focused his attention on the other man.

Costain gestured towards the two weapons invitingly. "I think you will find their weights comparable."

Sir Antony reached for the thin blade nearest him and gave it two expert twists of the wrist. He backed away from the table with a nod.

Costain picked up his own sword and faced the baronet. He smiled and saluted with three quick, smooth motions of his blade. Sir Antony returned the salute without emotion.

Lizzie pressed back against the door at the first clink of metal on metal and wished fervently that she had obeyed Sir Antony and left.

The two men tested each other warily. Costain proved quickest, and he slid swiftly and gracefully, his sword tip edging closer and closer with every lunge. Upon his lips hung an ever present snarl of contempt.

Sir Antony's expression remained stony. He parried each new attack smoothly, but he was rooted to the ground and clumsy on his feet.

Costain drove his body forward suddenly. Extending his arm, he skipped past his opponent. Sir Antony blocked the running attack and retreated.

The sides switched again and again and Lizzie drew into the farthest corner of the room as the shuffle of booted feet on hard wood, the grating of iron, the crash of furniture and the increasingly harsh breathing grew monstrously loud. She shrank back and watched the scene in horror. The minutes dragged on and on, and she closed her eyes, but the fascination was too great. She had to watch.

Costain lunged repeatedly and Sir Antony parried each thrust to the side, but his defence grew weaker under the other man's untiring onslaught. Short steps brought the men together, and Costain danced upon the balls of his feet, smelling his victory.

The baronet advanced at the wrong time as Costain executed a straight thrust forward. Sir Antony recovered and blocked his opponent's point, but was too late to stop himself before his foot caught against the rung of a fallen chair and he tripped.

Costain's blade sought its advantage and slipped forward again. The baronet ducked to one side with amazing swiftness as the razor-sharp edge passed an inch above his chest. His arm shot up and drove Costain's wide.

In one fluid motion, Sir Antony sprang into a crouch, rolled back upon his feet and lunged forward. His sword drove deep into the other's right shoulder.

He slowly withdrew the blade as Costain's smile disappeared completely and he dropped to the floor on his knees.

"I'll have the landlord fetch a doctor," Sir Antony said coldly.

"No need." The door swung open and Lord Croyton entered serenely and announced, "I thought we might have other uses for his services so I brought him back with me. Clever of me, what?"

He stepped aside lanquidly and allowed a small, mousy man entrance. The doctor took in the scene and shook his head but knelt beside his patient mutely.

Lizzie, quivering with relief, observed the final engagement with wide eyes. She now found herself staring with even wider eyes at Sir Antony.

There was no change in his expression except for the firm clenching of his jaw that tightened the already severe line of his mouth. He still gripped a blood-tipped sword in his right hand and her heart climbed into her throat as her breathing became shallow and quick. In a second, he towered before her, holding her immobile with his eyes alone.

"Lizzie—" his voice rang out, deep and angry "—I've been a damn fool."

His free arm encircled her waist and jerked her towards him. He bent slightly and crushed his lips upon hers with a fierceness that sent her heart flying faster and faster. Her hands moved slowly up his arms, conscious of every taut muscle as the warmth inside her exploded with the harsh beat of his breath upon her cheek. Every chill and fear vanished as she strained up against him. Her lips responded to his touch; her body moulded itself to his and, with a soft sigh, she entwined her arms about his neck and drew him down even closer.

He pulled away abruptly.

Unable to bear to destroy the dream, Lizzie inhaled deeply before opening her eyes.

He grinned sheepishly and his blue eyes twinkled into hers. It was Tony! *Her Tony!* Tears of joy filled her eyes instantly.

"Oh, Tony, I missed you so," she confessed in a whisper.

In response, he leaned his head towards hers again. Lizzie's eyes closed instinctively and her lips parted in breathless anticipation as a gentle caress brushed across them and passed slowly along the curve of her cheek. Into her ear came a hot breath.

"Maybe," Sir Antony returned, "when we're married, I will allow you to tell me what I can and cannot do. But that, my love, is only a maybe."

A laugh gurgled within her throat. "Oh, Tony," she pleaded, "just kiss me again."

Sensing this to be a very reasonable request, the baronet complied immediately.

"He canna stay here!" The landlord repeated adamantly.

"He shouldn't be moved" was the physician's rejoinder. "You've lost a great deal of blood, sir. The wound is a clean one and should heal in no time. It's just a matter of where to put ye," he explained and glared at the inn's proprietor.

"Put me in my carriage; I'll be fine," requested Costain.

At these words, Lord Croyton's attention was drawn from the amorous couple in the corner to the argument around him.

"Nonsense," he scolded and lounged against the table. "You heard the doctor. You'd probably bleed to death before you were a mile from here."

"Your concern is touching," scoffed Costain. "I'm certain it wouldn't matter to you one way or the other."

"On the contrary, it matters a great deal. I have no intention of allowing you, sir, to turn my future brother-in-law into a murderer. You will stay here."

All objections were halted by an upraised hand and Lord Croyton pulled his purse from a pocket, and extracting several coins, placed them in the landlord's palm.

"See that a room is made available immediately. My friend—" he paused to consider the word "—is to stay here as long as is necessary to recuperate fully. Any questions?"

The landlord counted the coins quickly. There was more than enough to cover the cost of room and board for one gentleman for well over a month.

"No questions, milord," he replied.

"Good."

"Damn you, Drenview." Costain felt the pinch of this new condescension and argued belligerently, "Do you expect me to thank you for your generosity?"

Lord Croyton studied him closely through his quizzing glass. "No, I don't," he remarked thoughtfully as the lens fell. "In fact, it is I who should be thanking you."

"What?"

The earl was now preoccupied with tapping the lid of a silver snuffbox. "Yes, quite," he finally replied. "You've managed to do in three short weeks what I haven't been able to do in—bless me!—more than three years. Surprising, I never considered jealousy before—monstrously shortsighted of me." He took a tiny pinch and added briskly, "Although when I suggested that you try again elsewhere, I meant elsewhere! Not my own sister!"

Costain rose with the doctor's assistance and faced the peer with a hard stare. "That episode has yet to be closed satisfactorily," he warned. "I trust you realize that fact."

"Really, dear boy," moaned his lordship, "I realize it all too well. It was, after all, my responsibility to fight you tonight, but Sir Antony was so keen on it that I couldn't bear to disappoint him. No hard feelings there, I trust?" He removed an invisible speck of dust from his sleeve and sniffed.

"No," admitted Costain. "No hard feelings there."

"Good. I hoped you would see it my way. As to the other matter, perhaps someday...not too soon. You must allow me time to practice, what?" He grinned weakly.

Costain smiled mirthlessly in return and permitted himself to be removed upstairs without further protests.

Lord Croyton surveyed the parlour forlornly. Two chairs, knocked over in the course of the duel, now lay upon the floor, but little other damage was apparent.

"What a mess," he muttered and his eyes focussed on his sister and Sir Antony. He sidestepped a fallen chair and casually strolled over to them.

"Tony..." he began.

There was no answer.

"I say, Tony," he said again with a frown, but netted no response.

His voice grew increasingly strident. "Really, Tony, I must protest strenu—"

The sword in Sir Antony's hand shot up, and Lord Croyton blinked to discover its bloody point within inches of his face. Cautiously, the earl extracted a perfumed linen handkerchief from his sleeve and raised it to his nose.

"Odd's fish, sir," he complained, "you know how I feel about blood!"

"What do you protest, Reggie?" Sir Antony demanded.

His lordship blinked again at the hard voice. "Yes, well, I suppose we can disregard the protest," he decided amicably, "but I'm afraid I really must ask your intentions."

"I intend to marry your sister, sir" was the answer.

"Well, yes, I know *that*," he returned peevishly.

"You don't object?"

The sword fell slightly, and his lordship seized the opportunity this indecision presented. With linen between himself and the deadly blade, he gently guided it aside.

"It grieves me that you persist so in this folly—" he sighed "—but if you will recall, I've never objected to your marryin' Lizzie—merely to the length of time it's taken you to get around to it."

Sir Antony tossed the sword to the floor, shamefaced. "Sorry, Reggie," he apologized.

"Now, then—" Lord Croyton heaved another long-suffering sigh "—will you do me the honour of answerin' my question?"

Sir Antony stared at him blankly.

His sleepy blue eyes rolled upwards and he gestured openly. "Your intentions?" he repeated. "Now that we've concluded this frightfully hectic romance, might I ask when we are to return to London and—" he glanced despairingly about the room "—civilisation?"

Sir Antony barked wth laughter. "We're not," he said succinctly.

"Beg pardon?" his lordship enquired with both eyebrows raised.

He did not receive an answer to his query as Sir Antony concentrated upon the woman in his arms and kissed her once. "Until tonight," he said, "I never truly considered it possible to lose you. Or what it would mean to me if I did. You were always there—always mine—despite any argument. I apologize for that, but I won't compromise, Lizzie."

Her heart beat wildly in her throat as Lizzie searched Sir Antony's eyes for some clue to his meaning. All she saw was the determination and will which were so new to her, and a tiny but very pleasant shiver ran up her spine.

"I've made too many mistakes not to recognize that the worst one would be to let you go," he continued, "but we can't keep arguing at cross purposes for the same thing. I know what I want, and I won't settle for getting it any way other than my own. Realize that fact, accept it, and take or leave it now. Lizzie, I love you. *Will* you marry me?"

Lizzie leaned against him and conceded softly, "Yes, I'll wait another year."

"Don't be silly. We're heading north tonight—" the words were crisp and clear "—to Gretna Green."

If Sir Antony had thought she might object, he was proved wrong.

"Oh, Tony! Yes!" she cried and flung her arms about his neck.

"North? Gretna Green? Damme!"

"You may come with us if you like, Reggie—" Sir Antony spoke softly, kissing Lizzie tenderly between each sentence "—or stay here, but either way we're going. It would be grand if you came. You could give the bride away and be best man at the same time. We'd like to have you there, wouldn't we, love?"

"Oh, yes," murmured Lizzie. "Do come, Reggie."

Their lack of enthusiasm was not lost upon the earl, and he soon wondered if they even remembered that he was waiting. He sighed and picked up the chair at his feet and had just succeeded in righting it when the landlord returned.

That auspicious innkeeper surveyed the room with nearly the same degree of dismay as Lord Croyton had previously. His eyes travelled from the couple to the bored-looking dandy and back again.

Sensing the man's helplessness, his lordship once more pulled out his purse and retrieved two coins.

"If I've learned anythin' over the past few weeks," he said, "it is that when the opportunity arises, sir, one must seize it." He dropped the coins onto the table and commanded, "My good man, a bottle of your best claret and something to eat—I'm not particular. This—" he gestured to the monies "—should, I trust, more than cover the food and—" he made a breezy movement to indicate the remainder of the room "—incidentals."

The landlord pocketed the coins. "Your Lordship is most generous," he said, bowing obsequiously. "The best of the house is yours."

He halted before departing, however, long enough to admire the young couple. "Ah, love," he whispered, for he was at heart a romantic soul, "isn't it wonderful, sir?"

His lordship dismissed this sentimentality with a coarse sniff. "Love is not the product of a sane mind," he proclaimed, and continued his discourse with fervent disgust. "To be cavorting pell-mell across the length and breadth of England without thought to sleep or—more important—where the next repast may be found, isn't natural! And when I think—" he reached down to knock a clod of dirt from his boot "—on the state of my wardrobe, I positively shudder! No, sir, love is most definitely the curse of an insane mind! Brought on, no doubt, by lack of sleep and an inadequate diet."

The landlord fled.

Lord Croyton dropped into a chair with a small sigh. "I only hope," he added, unheedful of the fact that no one was listening, "'tis not contagious."

Harlequin Regency Romance™

COMING NEXT MONTH

#27 ENTERPRISING LADY by Eva Rutland
Lydia Crenshaw had a terrible secret. If the ton were to find out, she would be ruined. The last thing she needed was to fall in love with a duke who was notoriously known for escaping wedded bliss. And when he discovered her terrible secret, Lydia knew she had to take desperate measures.

#28 THE DIRTY FROG by Gwyneth Moore
Valentina Ashford and Charles de Michel were at daggers drawn from the moment they met. It didn't help that Valentina owed him for the very roof over her head. When Charles was arrested, Valentina was devastated but the surprise to follow was even more shocking. She had wanted to tell him her true feelings and refused to believe he would never come back.

Indulge a Little
Give a Lot

A LITTLE SELF-INDULGENCE CAN DO
A WORLD OF GOOD!

Last fall readers indulged themselves with fine romance and free gifts during the Harlequin®/ Silhouette® "Indulge A Little—Give A Lot" promotion. For every specially marked book purchased, 5¢ was donated by Harlequin/ Silhouette to Big Brothers/Big Sisters Programs and Services in the United States and Canada. We are pleased to announce that your participation in this unique promotion resulted in a total contribution of *$100,000.*

*

Watch for details on Harlequin® and Silhouette®'s next exciting promotion in September.

HARLEQUIN'S "BIG WIN"
SWEEPSTAKES RULES & REGULATIONS
NO PURCHASE NECESSARY TO ENTER OR RECEIVE A PRIZE

1. To enter and join the Reader Service, scratch off the metallic strips on all your BIG WIN tickets #1-#6. This will reveal the values for each sweepstakes entry number, the number of free book(s) you will receive, and your free bonus gift as part of our Reader Service. If you do not wish to take advantage of our Reader Service, but wish to enter the Sweepstakes only, scratch off the metallic strips on your BIG WIN tickets #1-#4. Return your entire sheet of tickets intact. Incomplete and/or inaccurate entries are ineligible for that section or sections of prizes. Not responsible for mutilated or unreadable entries or inadvertent printing errors. Mechanically reproduced entries are null and void.

2. Whether you take advantage of this offer or not, your Sweepstakes numbers will be compared against a list of winning numbers generated at random by the computer. In the event that all prizes are not claimed by March 31, 1992, a random drawing will be held from all qualified entries received from March 30, 1990 to March 31, 1992, to award all unclaimed prizes. All cash prizes (Grand to Sixth), will be mailed to the winners and are payable by cheque in U.S. funds. Seventh prize to be shipped to winners via third-class mail. These prizes are in addition to any free, surprise or mystery gifts that might be offered. Versions of this sweepstakes with different prizes of approximate equal value may appear in other mailings or at retail outlets by Torstar Corp. and its affiliates.

3. The following prizes are awarded in this sweepstakes: ★ Grand Prize (1) $1,000,000; First Prize (1) $25,000; Second Prize (1) $10,000; Third Prize (5) $5,000; Fourth Prize (10) $1,000; Fifth Prize (100) $250; Sixth Prize (2500) $10; ★★ Seventh Prize (6000) $12.95 ARV.

   ★ This Sweepstakes contains a Grand Prize offering of $1,000,000 annuity. Winner will receive $33,333.33 a year for 30 years without interest totalling $1,000,000.

   ★★ Seventh Prize: A fully illustrated hardcover book published by Torstar Corp. Approximate value of the book is $12.95.

   Entrants may cancel the Reader Service at any time without cost or obligation to buy (see details in center insert card).

4. This promotion is being conducted under the supervision of Marden-Kane, Inc., an independent judging organization. By entering this Sweepstakes, each entrant accepts and agrees to be bound by these rules and the decisions of the judges, which shall be final and binding. Odds of winning in the random drawing are dependent upon the total number of entries received. Taxes, if any, are the sole responsibility of the winners. Prizes are nontransferable. All entries must be received by no later than 12:00 NOON, on March 31, 1992. The drawing for all unclaimed sweepstakes prizes will take place May 30, 1992, at 12:00 NOON, at the offices of Marden-Kane, Inc., Lake Success, New York.

5. This offer is open to residents of the U.S., the United Kingdom, France and Canada, 18 years or older except employees and their immediate family members of Torstar Corp., its affiliates, subsidiaries, Marden-Kane, Inc., and all other agencies and persons connected with conducting this Sweepstakes. All Federal, State and local laws apply. Void wherever prohibited or restricted by law. Any litigation respecting the conduct and awarding of a prize in this publicity contest may be submitted to the Régie des loteries et courses du Québec.

6. Winners will be notified by mail and may be required to execute an affidavit of eligibility and release which must be returned within 14 days after notification or, an alternative winner may be selected. Canadian winners will be required to correctly answer an arithmetical skill-testing question administered by mail which must be returned within a limited time. Winners consent to the use of their names, photographs and/or likenesses for advertising and publicity in conjunction with this and similar promotions without additional compensation.

7. For a list of our major winners, send a stamped, self-addressed envelope to: WINNERS LIST c/o MARDEN-KANE, INC., P.O. BOX 701, SAYREVILLE, NJ 08871. Winners Lists will be fulfilled after the May 30, 1992 drawing date.

If Sweepstakes entry form is missing, please print your name and address on a 3" × 5" piece of plain paper and send to:

In the U.S.
Harlequin's "BIG WIN" Sweepstakes
901 Fuhrmann Blvd.
P.O. Box 1867
Buffalo, NY 14269-1867

In Canada
Harlequin's "BIG WIN" Sweepstakes
P.O. Box 609
Fort Erie, Ontario
L2A 5X3

© 1989 Harlequin Enterprises Limited   Printed in the U.S.A.

LTY-H590

Have You Been Introduced To
THE GENTLEMAN
Yet?

If you enjoyed Dorothy Glenn's THE HELL RAISER (HH #45), you won't want to miss its companion book, THE GENTLEMAN, by Kristin James.

As a boy, Stephen Ferguson was taken away from his brother and his western home, then raised with all the comforts that money and city society could provide. As a man, he longed to be reunited with the family he'd nearly forgotten. In THE GENTLEMAN (HH #43) Stephen finds not only his father and brother but something even more precious—the love of a woman who is every inch his opposite—and absolutely his perfect match!

THE LOVES OF A CENTURY...

Join American Romance in a nostalgic look back at the Twentieth Century—at the lives and loves of American men and women from the turn-of-the-century to the dawn of the year 2000.

Journey through the decades from the dance halls of the 1900s to the discos of the seventies ... from Glenn Miller to the Beatles ... from Valentino to Newman ... from corset to miniskirt ... from beau to Significant Other.

Relive the moments ... recapture the memories.

Look for the CENTURY OF AMERICAN ROMANCE series starting next month in Harlequin American Romance. In one of the four American Romance titles appearing each month, for the next twelve months, we'll take you back to a decade of the Twentieth Century, where you'll relive the years and rekindle the romance of days gone by.

Don't miss a day of the CENTURY OF AMERICAN ROMANCE.

The women...the men...the passions...
the memories....